WATCH

THE

SKY

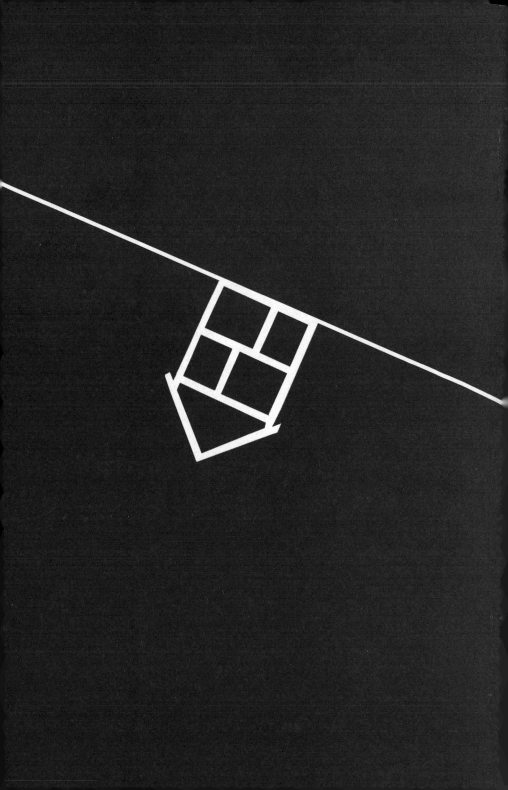

"It's my fault," Jory said. "I said she could wear her slippers. I know better."

"So does Kit." Caleb's eyes frowned. "There's not much I ask of you, my family. But everything I *do* ask is for a reason. Go fetch your boots, Kit. We'll wait."

Kit puffed out her cheeks, silent as ever.

Caleb had little patience for Kit's silence. Sometimes he would ask her questions, knowing she wouldn't answer. "It's because she's got nothing inside her head," he'd say, not quite serious, not quite joking.

Jory knew that wasn't true—Kit had an imagination twice the size of Jory's. Anyone who watched their games would know that. Like pressing flowers between book pages, a game they called Naturemaking. Or spreading Kit's flowered blanket in the fields for Cloudwatching—even if his sister didn't speak, Jory liked to guess the cumulus creatures she had in mind. Or painting wooden houses for Worldbuilding, their favorite game of all.

"Go on," Jory said under his breath, and Kit scurried off. She returned a couple of minutes later, clad in combats like the rest of them.

"Good," Caleb said. "Let's all have a seat."

Jory knelt against the wall, and Kit sat cross-legged beside him. The chill from the concrete floor seeped into his knees.

"Shall we open it?" Caleb held up the newspaper.

The family nodded.

faces aglow in the lantern light. Caleb preferred lanterns to electric lamps. Another kind of "practice"—though he never said for what. But the shivering lights produced an atmospheric effect. They made Caleb's every word seem profound.

"'Morning, my birds," Mom said.

She'd brushed and braided her hair into a tidy, honey-colored rope. Ansel, Jory's toddler brother, slept on her lap, his face buried in the crook of her arm.

Caleb smiled at the family. Not with his mouth—with his eyes. Caleb's eyes did all the expressing for his face, since his dense beard covered the rest of it. He had big round shoulders and what Mom called soldier's hands: strong, cal-lused, capable. Jory felt safe with him around.

Except when he spoke about signs.

"Everybody's here? Good, that's good." Caleb nodded at Jory, appraising him. Then he turned to Kit. "Where are your boots?"

Jory squeezed Kit's hand, feeling annoyed with himself. He should have insisted she wear them. Even though Kit had no need for them. She never went anywhere, not even to school. Mom homeschooled Kit, just like she used to homeschool Jory.

But boots were one of Caleb's orders. Caleb wasn't a violent man. He rarely even raised his voice. But he'd been a soldier in a desert war Jory didn't know much about, and Jory didn't want to test his temper.

giving orders—mostly camouflaged as suggestions.

It's good practice to keep our boots beside our beds. Just in case.

It's best not to speak to our neighbors.

The old barn isn't a safe place for children.

We should all keep an eye out for signs.

The *whys*, however, were much more rare. Like what the signs were *for*.

Jory hoped intuition would explain it. The same intuition that steered him toward signs in the first place. Once Caleb *just knew* he'd found a sign, he'd *just know* what the sign meant, too.

Which sounded good. But it also made Jory anxious. Sometimes his shoulders felt heavy by the end of the day, burdened by anticipation of any sudden certainty.

Because signs could be anything.

A car engine late at night. A squirrel corpse rotting on the side of the road with maggots in its eyes. Lights in the sky at twilight—*always watch the sky*, Caleb said.

Because signs could be *anything*.

—

Jory led Kit into the farmhouse's patio. That's what they called it, even though it wasn't a real patio—there was no way outside. The single sliding door was padlocked shut.

Mom and Caleb sat in the Adirondack chairs, their

assembly. "But we don't get to decide these things. Now, hurry up." He motioned to Kit's boots.

Ignoring him, Kit jammed on her ballet slippers, the ones she'd been wearing the morning Jory had found her in the pumpkin field. Now they were tattered and dirty, splattered with paint. She wound herself in her flowered blanket and looked at him.

"What?" he said.

She stared harder, in that wordless way of hers.

"Is it a sign, you mean?" Jory shrugged. "I don't know. It might be."

—

Signs were everywhere.

Everywhere and anywhere, Caleb said. That was the problem. They came at any time. And they could be almost anything.

Red leaves in the springtime. Pages torn from a library book. All the fish in an aquarium facing the same way. A cracked egg with twin yolks.

"How do you know?" Jory had asked his stepdad once. "I mean, how do you know you're seeing a sign? Instead of a bunch of coincidental fish?"

"You'll just know," Caleb had replied.

Caleb was fickle with explanations. Sometimes he shared them. Sometimes he didn't. But he had no problem them: combat boots with thick, ridged soles. Caleb, Jory's stepdad called boots a man's best friend. Jory never saw him without his. Sometimes they were dirt-caked in the morning, as if he spent all night working in the moonlit fields out back.

Jory grabbed his flashlight, then hurried to his sister's room. The family's old farmhouse had low, sloped ceilings and narrow, creaky hallways. It seemed built for tunneling creatures instead of people, like the rabbit warrens he'd read about at school.

"Kit?" Jory knocked twice, then opened her door. His sister's bed was made, but she wasn't in it. "Kit?" he tried again.

She flung herself at him, all elbows and blackbird hair, nearly knocking him off his feet. Jory laughed and pushed her away. She spun twice and came to a stop, grinning, her pink cheeks in full bloom.

He shouldn't have been surprised she was awake. Kit was three years younger than Jory and had a way of knowing things.

"We've got another family meeting," he told her. "You've probably guessed."

She rolled her eyes. They were so large, Jory could practically hear their movement.

"I *know*," he said, messing up her dark hair. It was impossible to get a good night's sleep, not knowing whether Mom might jostle them awake for an early-morning

SIGNS

FOR THE THIRD TIME IN OCTOBER, Mom woke Jory before dawn.

"It's arrived," she told him.

Jory sat up in bed, rubbing a dream from his eyes. It was gone already; all he could remember was darkness. "Is it a sign?"

"It's the paper." Mom still wore her sleep-wrinkled nightdress, and her hair hung loose, unbrushed. Jory hadn't seen her this disheveled since she'd worked overtime at the coffee shop. "Wake your sister and meet us on the patio, okay? Bring a light."

"But is it a sign? The paper?"

"I don't know." She leaned in and kissed his forehead. "It might be."

Once the door closed, Jory kicked away his covers and stuffed his feet into his boots. The whole family wore

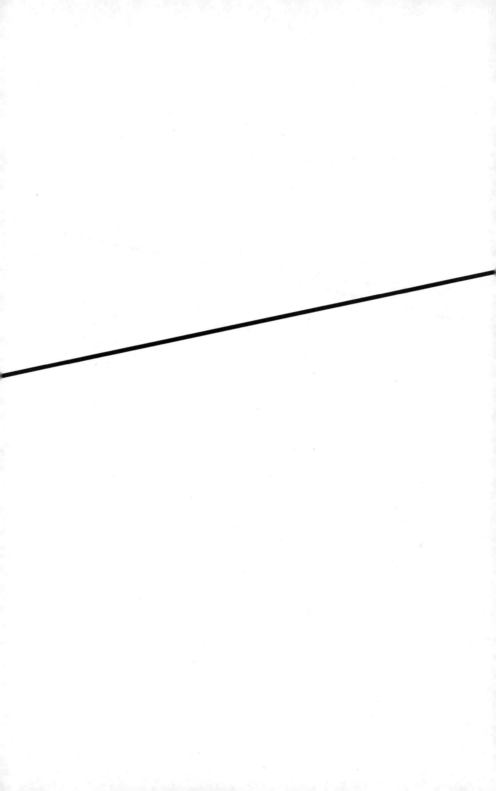

FOR MY (NOT SO SECRET) SISTER

FIRST EDITION, APRIL 2015
1 2 3 4 5 6 7 8 9 10
G475-5664-5-15015
PRINTED IN THE UNITED STATES OF AMERICA
THIS BOOK IS SET IN 11.5 PT. JANSON TEXT
DESIGNED BY WHITNEY MANGER

LIBRARY OF CONGRESS CATALOGING-IN-PUBLICATION DATA
HUBBARD, KIRSTEN.
WATCH THE SKY / KIRSTEN HUBBARD.—FIRST EDITION.
PAGES CM
SUMMARY: "THE SIGNS ARE EVERYWHERE. ACCCORDING TO JORY'S STEPFATHER, CALEB. THE END IS COMING, AND THEY MUST BE PRE-PARED. SCHOOL IS JORY'S ONLY ESCAPE FROM CALEB'S TIGHT GRASP, AND WITH THE HELP OF NEW FRIENDS, HE BEGINS TO EXPLORE A WORLD BEYOND HIS FAMILY'S DESERT RANCH"—PROVIDED BY PUBLISHER.
ISBN 978-1-4847-0833-0 (HARDBACK)
[1. FAMILY LIFE—FICTION. 2. STEPFATHERS—FICTION. 3. PROPHECIES—FICTION. 4. SELF-RELIANCE—FICTION.]   I. TITLE.
PZ7.H8584WAT 2015
[FIC]—DC23   2014042086

REINFORCED BINDING
VISIT WWW.DISNEYBOOKS.COM

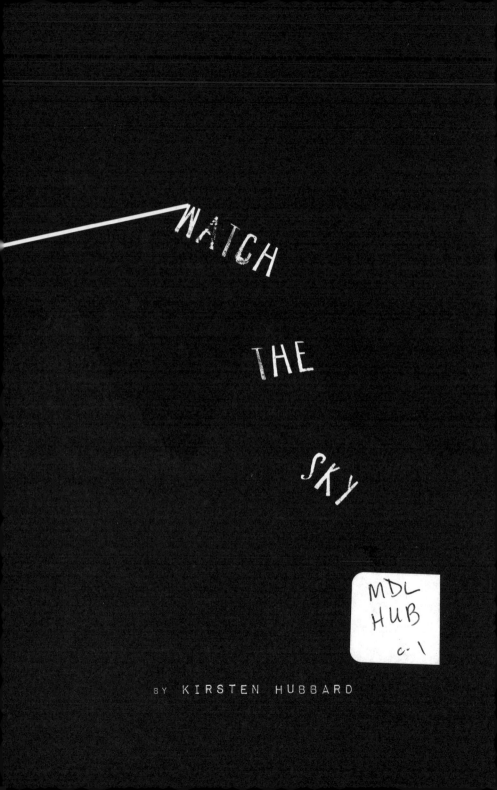

WATCH THE SKY

BY KIRSTEN HUBBARD

Disney • HYPERION   LOS ANGELES   NEW YORK

Ceremoniously, he unfolded the paper and shook it open. Jory saw what looked like stale white icing drizzled all over the pages. In some places, it covered entire paragraphs. Caleb scratched with his thumbnail, and the white came off in a fine powder, but the words underneath were still impossible to read.

"Well, that's that. It's a sign if I've ever seen one."

"Are you sure?" Mom asked.

"I'm certain."

A sign. For certain. Jory felt his heart leap and his stomach drop simultaneously. *Pick one or the other*, he ordered his middle. "A sign of what?"

"Communication's the first thing to go—" Mom began.

"That's right," Caleb interrupted. "They should have taught you that in school. What are they teaching kids nowadays, if not what to watch out for?"

He looked at Jory like he expected an answer.

"Um . . . pre-algebra?" Jory replied. "Social studies?"

"Anyway," Caleb continued, "it's a sign. I'm certain. I just don't know if it's the one we've been waiting for."

He stared at the paper daubed in white. He stared and stared, until Kit's sleepy head came to rest on Jory's shoulder. Jory looked out the window to keep himself awake. The old barn carved a dark, angular shape in the early morning light. His old broken bicycle leaned against it. Beyond, the fields were golden-gray.

Finally, Caleb leaned back in his seat.

"It's just not enough. Not yet."

Mom made a small sound of disappointment. "Are you sure?"

He nodded. "When it's the right time, we'll know. We won't have any doubts."

Jory felt disappointed, too. When Caleb was excited, he was *electric*, charging the air and igniting the entire family's mood. When he wasn't, the house seemed darker and narrower.

"We've just been planning for so long . . ." Mom said.

"We have. But even so, we're not ready yet. Not even close." Caleb began to fold the paper neatly, then changed his mind and crumpled it into a ball. He stood. "We should be thankful for every last hour we have, my family. When they arrive—when it finally happens, there'll be no time left." He nodded at Kit and Jory, touched Ansel's cheek, and then disappeared inside the house.

"When *who* arrive?" Jory asked Mom quietly.

"When it's safe for us to know, Caleb will tell us. Now, get some sleep, both of you." She paused thoughtfully, smoothing back Ansel's hair. "While you still have the chance."

●

THE SECRET SISTER

JORY KNEW HIS FAMILY WAS DIFFERENT FROM OTHER FAMILIES.

In books, that sort of thing usually involved immortality or magic powers at puberty or something. None of which seemed true for Jory—although from time to time, he stared in the mirror and wondered.

No, Jory's family was a *different* kind of different. He'd always suspected it, but returning to real school last year had confirmed it.

Most kids had friends they hung out with after school. Most kids had mothers who left the house more than every couple of weeks. Most kids had siblings who spoke. And Jory never asked, but he was pretty sure nobody had stepdads who constantly talked about signs.

And secrets.

Sometimes Jory felt like he lived in a maze, with walls

blocking off the best directions. There were just *so many secrets*. Secrets from him. Secrets from Kit. Secrets from the rest of the world.

As far as he could tell, they all boiled down to this:

Caleb knew something.

Something big.

Something the family needed to prepare for.

That's all Caleb had ever told them. Waiting for the facts, the details, the *answers*, was frustrating for Jory. But Mom promised and re-promised that Caleb would explain everything in good time. When it was safe.

Keeping the family safe was Caleb's main concern.

Out of all the families in the world, Caleb had chosen Jory's family to protect. He had chosen them to make his own, to spend his time and money on. Unlike Jory's real father, who had chosen himself. He'd left for the city when Jory was five years old. "I'll call when I get there," he'd said, squatting down to Jory's height. Then he'd walked past Mom and out the door.

For nearly a year, the family was just Jory and Mom.

Then it was Jory, Mom, and Caleb. Ansel came later.

Kit came first.

———

The first time Jory saw Kit, she was eating a pumpkin.

Actually, before that, she was knocking on pumpkins.

Jory had no idea she was going to *eat* one. If he had, he might have said something sooner.

It was nearly three years ago; Jory was nine, so Kit was around six. He was heading out to check on the winter melons when he glimpsed her, creeping through the desiccated vines in nothing but overalls and ballet slippers. From time to time, she'd crouch down and rap her knuckles on one of the half-rotten, waxy orange globes.

After a while, she stopped, settling on one particular pumpkin. She prodded the toe of her slipper in the dirt. Then she leaned over and clawed out a stone. She knelt again, raised her arm, and bashed the stone into the pumpkin.

I should probably say something, Jory thought. Like *Excuse me! That's not your pumpkin*, or *Leave that poor pumpkin alone!* Except less stupid-sounding. But he was captivated.

When the girl pulled out the stone, a smile-shaped gash remained. She grinned right back. Then, as Jory watched, she slammed the stone into the pumpkin over and over, with what seemed like enough force to snap her skinny arms. She was stronger than she looked. Finally, a chunk of pumpkin flesh broke off, the color of canned macaroni.

She shoved her small fist inside the hole and withdrew a handful of seed and guts.

And then she ate them.

Before Mom married Caleb, Jory had eaten plenty of disgusting things—mostly from the "Nobody wants these!" section at the supermarket. Vienna sausages. Imitation abalone. Expired onion soup. He hadn't really minded, it was like a game they played, sampling the world's strangest foods. Raw pumpkin beat them all, though. The gluey tendrils, the slimy seeds . . .

Before he knew it, he was jogging over to her.

"Hey!" he called.

She froze, one arm still stuffed inside the pumpkin. Her dark hair stuck up in every direction, like rumpled blackbird feathers. Her eyes were enormous.

"Do you need something to eat?"

Silently, she stared at him.

"We have plenty of food. You don't have to eat—that." He tried not to wrinkle his nose at the disemboweled pumpkin. "My family's house is right there. Come on, I'll take you."

Jory held out his hand. She stared at it. "It's okay," he said. He started to wonder if she was right in the head. "My family's nice. Really."

After a moment, she took his hand. Hers was sticky.

"What's your name?" he asked.

"Kit," she whispered.

That was all she ever said.

—

"Are you sure Kit's my sister?" Jory asked time and again. At least he knew what name to call her.

"Of course she is," Mom always replied. "You're my son, and she's my daughter. Which makes her your sister. And you her brother."

"But how do you know for certain?"

"Mothers know their children, Jory. I'd recognize your voice in a chorus. I could find you in a crowd of thousands. A mother's love is an invisible cord, linking her children heart to heart."

Which was sweet, but it didn't exactly answer his question. *Any* of his questions. Like where had she come from? Where had she been? Why had she taken so long to arrive?

What's more, Kit didn't look like Jory. His hair was light brown, while hers was nearly black. In a certain light, her brown eyes *sort of* looked hazel, like Jory's. Her olive skin was several shades darker than his, though Mom said she was just suntanned.

"Your sister's come a long way," she said.

How far, Kit never told them. She never spoke at all. She never laughed or cried. She never even whimpered. If Jory hadn't heard Kit speak in the pumpkin field, he wouldn't have believed she knew how.

Mom didn't seem to mind, though. It only made her more determined to care for Kit. "She's been through a lot," she said. "She *needs* us. Even if she can't use words to tell us."

Caleb, however, crossed his arms before he opened

them. Jory remembered how his stepdad had watched Kit through squinted eyes, as if she were a curiosity, an alien moonstone fallen from the sky.

"We don't know where she's been," Caleb said. "Or who might be looking for her. I don't want to compromise the safety of this family."

"But what about Kit's safety?" Mom asked. "Nobody can keep her safe like we can."

Mom rarely asked for anything, but she asked for Kit. And finally, Caleb conceded. "As long as she behaves," he said. "And as long as Jory can keep her a secret, until we know more about her."

A secret sister!

How fun—and also, how strange. But lots of things in Jory's life were strange. Like the locked barn, and the neighbor ladies who stared from across the canyon, and the unseen pests that kept dragging Mom's tomato plants underground. The *whole* plants! Even after Caleb sprinkled bonemeal to frighten them away.

It took Kit some time to adjust to family life, but Mom persisted. She braided Kit's hair and tucked wildflowers under the elastic. Painted her fingernails. Told hilarious girls-only stories invented just for her, while Jory giggled into his fist, pretending not to listen. Mom never minded how dirty Kit and Jory got, playing in the fields, leaping and tumbling, dancing together until they got so dizzy, they watched the sky spin from their backs.

Kit was the center of the family's universe.

Then Ansel was born.

—

Mom delivered Ansel at home, with a midwife's help. She was a crabby, hunchbacked old woman—or so Mom said, since Jory never saw the midwife himself. Caleb made the kids wait in the patio, silent as field mice.

"Your mother needs to concentrate on creation," he said, then hurried away.

Keeping quiet was no problem for Kit, but that didn't mean she was unbothered. By then, Jory was a master at reading Kit's silent emotions. Her nails, gnawed to the quick. Her saucer-eyed stare. Her cheeks blooming pink. Usually, she was a galloping, bouncy bundle of energy, but not today.

"Mom'll be all right," Jory consoled her, after an hour of nibbling stale cinnamon grahams and pretending to color.

Kit bit her thumbnail.

"She—"

Jory's words were interrupted by a wail. He knelt on the floor beside Kit.

"That's just how it sounds," he explained, reassuring himself as much as her. "Having a baby. It hurts, but it's perfectly natural. The most natural thing of all. If you think about it, every person on planet Earth came from a mother."

Kit broke a graham cracker in half, then set both halves on the plate.

"And anyway, she's done it before, hasn't she? There's nothing to worry about . . ."

The sudden stillness was just as piercing as his mother's cry. Then came another wail—a new kind, high and shrill, like a field mouse stuck in a trap.

The door flew open so hard it bounced off the wall.

"A boy!" Caleb said triumphantly, his broad shoulders heaving with emotion. "Wash up and meet your brother." He hurried out.

"Now you've got two brothers," Jory told Kit. "That's something special."

All out of fingernails, Kit bit her lip.

—

Ansel really was something special. If *special* was the right word.

He was undersized from day one. Frail, with rice-paper skin, wispy hair, and pink-rimmed eyes, even when he wasn't crying. Mom spent most of her time tending to him. Time she'd once spent with Jory and Kit.

She still took care of Kit's lessons. But not Jory's, for long.

A few months after Ansel was born, Caleb informed Jory he'd be starting fifth grade in town. Mom found managing two kids' studies and nursing a fussy infant more trouble than she'd anticipated, especially with Caleb working long hours at the factory.

"But that's not the only reason," Caleb said. "It's safer this way."

"Safer?" Jory asked.

"I'll explain," Caleb said, to Jory's relief. "There are many reasons parents choose to homeschool kids. Overcrowded, underfunded schools. Quality of the curriculum. Religious beliefs. Some reasons are acceptable. Others aren't as acceptable. According to the Officials, anyway."

"The Officials?" Jory repeated. It wasn't the first time Caleb had mentioned them.

"They're everywhere," Caleb said. "In everybody's business. They want to regulate everything, including what parents teach their kids. To ensure all kids are being taught the correct way—inside the classroom, but also outside it."

"*Their* correct way," Mom added.

Caleb nodded. "The way the Officials think is correct. And because it's easier to regulate lessons inside the classroom, Officials pay closer attention to homeschooled families, especially as the children grow older. We don't need that extra attention on our family."

"In regular school, you can blend in," Mom said, rocking Ansel in her arms. "You'll look just like other kids."

"Exactly," Caleb said. "It's a way of hiding in plain sight."

"Hiding in plain sight," Jory repeated. It was an interesting concept.

Caleb nodded. "If we lived in a more remote area—in the desert east of here, maybe—it would be different. But we live in town. And we think you're old enough. Old enough to know when to listen, and when not to. Old enough to remember that school is school, and family is family. Can we trust you to keep our family's secrets?"

"Yes, sir," Jory replied. "Of course."

Jory figured Caleb was talking about Kit, but he didn't have to worry. Jory would never do anything to compromise the safety of his sister. Even if he had to pretend she didn't exist.

He worried for himself, though.

He hadn't gone to real school in years—not since before Mom married Caleb and they moved to the old farmhouse. Back when they lived in a tiny apartment on the industrial side of town, and Mom worked at that crummy coffee shop. Back when the pain of Dad leaving still throbbed like a skinned knee, an elbow whacked against a doorjamb, a blister he thought would never, ever heal.

It faded, though. Like every pain. Until Jory could barely remember.

School he remembered in bits and pieces. Dry-erase boards and desks in clusters. Classmates with blurry faces. Computer screens, bright enough to squint at. Toys in colorful plastic tubs, although fifth grade would probably have fewer toys than first.

Jory was excited.

But mostly terrified.

He tried not to blame Ansel. It wasn't anybody's fault, being born.

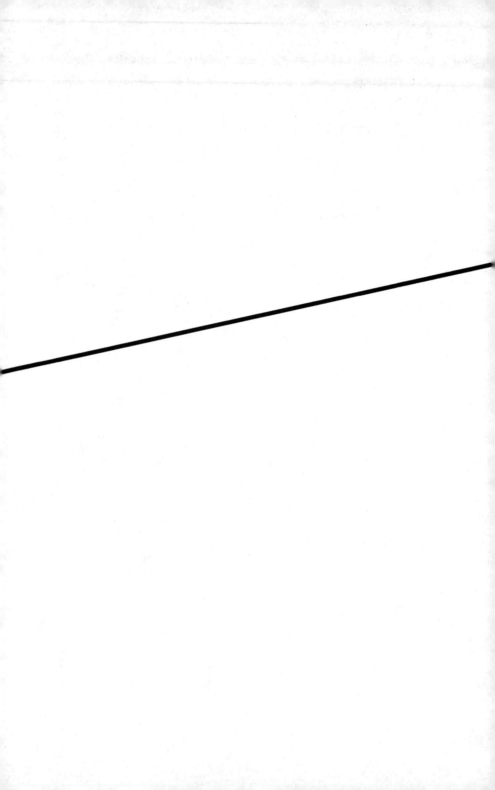

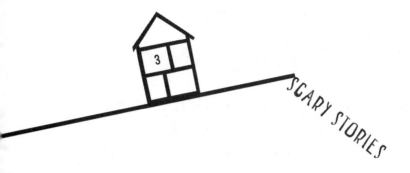

JORY LIKED SIXTH GRADE MUCH BETTER THAN FIFTH. Most of that was because of his teacher, Mr. Bradley.

Mr. Bradley had inch-long dimples and a booming voice, and was tall enough to spread his palm flat on the classroom's ceiling. He didn't even have to jump.

Today, he was discussing accidental mummies—the kind preserved in swamps and long-forgotten bogs. Like the Tollund Man in Denmark, and the Haraldskær Woman, who had probably been the victim of human sacrifice. Any reasonable person would be fascinated.

Most of Jory's classmates looked bored.

Erik Dixon slumped with his chin in his hand. Paisley Matthews yawned over and over. Alice Brooks-Diaz doodled on a sketchpad hidden in her social studies book. When she glanced up, Jory looked away quickly. Alice made him nervous.

Anyway, Jory didn't get it. He *liked* school, though he tried not to let it show too much. In sixth grade, some things were best kept hidden—like underpants, unless you were the low-jeans type.

He used to *love* school. Back when he believed his teachers.

Not that he disbelieved them now. He just knew better than to accept his lessons at face value. It was a matter of critical thinking. A matter of looking deeper. Thinking outside the box.

Caleb had taught him that last year, a few months after he'd started school. Jory had been telling Kit about the solar system when Caleb had touched his shoulder.

"Let's have a talk," he'd said. "Man to man."

Kit had rolled her eyes, but luckily Caleb hadn't seen it. Together, Jory and Caleb had strolled into the fields, tangled with pumpkin vines. Blue jays had gossiped in the canyon, even though the sky had looked wintry.

"I know your studies are exciting," Caleb had said. "You're exposed to so many things. New ideas. New ways of thinking."

Well, sure—that's what school was for, wasn't it?

"But you're a smart kid," he'd gone on, making Jory flush with pride. "Smarter than I was at your age. I just want to remind you to take everything with a grain of salt."

"What do you mean?" Jory had asked, perplexed.

"Don't accept everything you're told as true."

"But . . . why would my teachers lie to me?"

"They're not lying, *necessarily*." Caleb had scratched his beard. "In most cases, they *think* they're telling the truth. They're teaching what they've been taught—what their own teachers were taught, and so on. Over the years, the lies get mixed in."

"But what about the facts? Some things are just . . . *true*."

"Like what?"

"Like . . ." Jory had thought. "Benjamin Franklin signed the Declaration of Independence in 1776. And pandas like eating bamboo."

"What if somebody forged Benjamin Franklin's signature?" Caleb had asked. "I doubt there's video footage. And what if pandas only eat bamboo because that's all they have? What if they'd really prefer brussels sprouts?"

Jory had opened his mouth, then closed it.

Caleb had placed a hand on Jory's shoulder, smiling with his eyes. "It's just a matter of critical thinking. Looking deeper. Remember: you can't trust anyone but your family."

Ever since, Jory questioned everything his teachers said. A parade of *what ifs* marched endlessly through his head.

Like right now.

What if the Tollund Man was a hoax?

What if he wasn't even human? (He sure didn't look it.)

What if the Haraldskær Woman hadn't been sacrificed—she'd been an evil witch?

What if—

The bell rang, interrupting Jory's thoughts. "Start thinking about topics for your social studies projects," Mr. Bradley called as the class jostled for the door. "And be sure to look out for the meteor shower this weekend. It should be pretty spectacular!"

———

Jory took his time gathering his things. He hated lunchtime. In fifth grade, he'd sat with a couple of other loners, but this year they'd both joined the computer club, which met at lunch. Jory's family had no computer. Now he sat alone, at the very end of an endless table.

He used to sneak a book in his lap, until the day Erik Dixon had poked him in the shoulder.

"Whatchu readin'?"

Jory had lifted his book: *A Wrinkle in Time*, for class. "Just trying to get ahead," he mumbled. Which wasn't really true, since he'd read it twice already.

"Is that for school?" Erik had raised his eyebrows. "Lunch isn't for doing your homework, man. It's for hanging with your friends."

Erik was one of the nicer guys in the class. Almost too nice. An awkward silence had followed, as Jory waited for Erik to remember he didn't *have* any friends. He didn't trust anyone enough for that.

Especially not Alice Brooks-Diaz.

"I was reading a book of scary stories last night," Alice said. "It made me think of you, Jory Birch."

Jory wondered if he should be insulted. With Alice, it was hard to know.

Alice Brooks-Diaz had dark eyes, dark skin, and curly hair, which she sported in twin buns. It made her look like a baby koala. She always wore a red plaid jacket. It was so big, she had to shove back the cuffs every ten seconds. When she put on the hood, it swallowed her head.

She was one of those people everybody liked. The *magnetic* people, who attracted instead of repelled. She could sit anywhere she wanted—if she wanted. But every single day, halfway through lunch, Alice sat across from Jory.

And talked at him.

Not *to* him—that would involve more give and take. She talked *at* him. About the most random things. No matter how Jory reacted, she didn't seem to notice. Some days he gave one-word answers. Some days he ignored her. Some days, like yesterday, he got up and left without saying good-bye.

The next day, she'd sit across from him again.

Alice loved a good mystery, and Jory figured he was one of them. A mystery, or a riddle—one that only poking, prodding, and hours of never-ending chatter might solve.

"So this book of scary stories," Alice continued, shoving back her cuffs and tearing off a wedge of orange. "I thought of you because you like to read, obviously. But also, you live in a farmhouse, right? Is it haunted? I'd give *anything* to live in a haunted house. Bloody Marys in the mirrors and heartbeats under the floorboards, wow!"

"It isn't haunted," Jory said.

Alice leaned forward, encouraged by his muttered reply. "Are you sure? Sometimes you have no idea until you wake to a chalk-white face floating over your bed. They're always chalk-white in the stories—that's how you know they're ghosts."

"I told you, it isn't haunted. I've been living there five years. I'd know if there were ghosts."

"What about wormy old bodies?"

"I'm trying to eat," Jory said, pointing to his sandwich.

Alice stuffed an orange wedge in her mouth and kept on talking. "In the book I read, one of the stories had a secret passage. Like the Underground Railroad, except with monsters. Does your farmhouse have any of those, do you think?"

"No."

"Rooms behind the walls?" Alice tried. "Trapdoors? Locked closets?"

"None of our closets have locks."

"No locks anywhere?"

Jory shook his head. "Only on the barn."

"Wait—you have a barn? With a lock on it?"

He nodded.

Alice's eyes widened. "A locked barn? Wow! Your very own real-life mystery! I just *knew* you had one, Jory Birch. Is it filled with skeletons, do you think?"

He wished he hadn't said anything. "It's a really big lock," he said. "With a chain."

Alice leaned closer. "Maybe if we put our heads together, we can figure out a way to open it."

Jory didn't want to put his head anywhere near hers. Not because Alice wasn't pretty—*everyone* thought so, it wasn't just Jory—but because he couldn't trust her. He couldn't trust anyone at school. Only his family.

He stood up. "I've got to go."

"Okay. We'll talk more tomorrow!" She lowered her voice. "About the barn."

Tomorrow was Saturday, but he didn't feel like telling her.

———

Jory could walk home two ways: the short way down Vale Street, or the long way through the eucalyptus grove.

He always chose the long way.

First, because Alice and Erik both lived on Vale Street. Unless Jory got a head start, they'd be hanging with friends in their yards, which made him feel like dashing in the opposite direction. Even if Jory *did* have friends of his own, he wouldn't know what to talk about.

Second, because the Mendoza twins lived on Vale Street, too, and there was no way they'd let Jory pass by without some comment.

Hey, Farmer Jory, where's your tractor?

What's with the boots, tough guy?

The long way home took twice the time. But the houses were fewer, and nobody important lived in them. Also, Jory liked walking in the fragrant shade of the eucalyptus trees. They reminded him of koalas.

Not of Alice Brooks-Diaz—just koalas.

At last, he reached the edge of town. It wasn't farmland, exactly, but everybody who lived on the outskirts owned a few acres, and some people grew things. He saw the neighbor ladies' house, facing his family's farmhouse on the other side of the canyon. Sometimes Jory caught them watching as he and Kit played in the fields. Once, they'd even waved. Jory knew Caleb wouldn't approve, so he'd pretended not to see them.

As Jory crossed the bridge, he almost tripped over a black-and-white dog, which seemed to appear out of nowhere. It had long, wavy ears and a spiral for a tail.

"Get lost," he yelled, waving it away.

The dog barked at Jory, who felt offended. Even though he'd yelled at it first.

More eucalyptus trees shaded the back of the family's

property, along with a couple of oaks. At the edge of the road, Jory opened the rusty mailbox. He always checked the mail, since Mom didn't venture down to the road if she could help it. Nothing this time.

After the trees came the fields. Caleb grew crops like pumpkins, cucumbers, and tomatoes. They owned no animals, though Jory and Kit had dug up several square-shaped bells. There must have been goats once.

Where the fields ended, the canyon began.

It was a big canyon, all on its own. But it was just one finger in a massive network of canyons, branching into the desert and the city and beyond. A labyrinth of tangled brush. Caleb claimed you could follow the pleats all the way to the ocean—if you could avoid the infinite dead ends along the way.

Even though the canyon was technically in Jory's backyard, he wasn't allowed to explore it. It was off-limits. Filled with Danger, capital *D*.

Rattlesnakes.

Poison oak, which turned red in the summer and torched your skin.

Scorpions.

Spiders. Hairy ones.

Coyotes, who *yip yip yip*ped every time a siren wailed by on the highway.

The off-limits rule didn't bother Jory much. Like Mom, he wasn't the daring type. Standing at the canyon's edge felt wild enough. Especially at night, when he couldn't see the bottom, and the wind shuddered through the underbrush, and everything seemed to have eyes.

And then there was the barn.

The barn sat between the house and the canyon. It had been locked when the family moved in, with an angry-looking padlock and a rusty chain. The heavy, foreboding kind Jacob Marley lugged around in *A Christmas Carol*. The barn had never interested Jory. He'd always walked right by it, except when he paused to lean his old broken bike against the wall.

Today, he stopped and stared.

Then he kept walking, a little more quickly.

4

THERE'S SOMETHING ABOUT THAT MAN

WHEN JORY SHUFFLED INTO THE KITCHEN the next morning, the family was already up: Kit kneading dough for a loaf of bread, Mom scratching a graphite line on the doorjamb to document Ansel's height. A purple, fruity substance simmered on the stove, some kind of jelly.

"Is Caleb at work?" Jory asked.

Caleb had been working more than usual lately. Double shifts at the factory, where he operated massive, scary-sounding machines. Evenings in the fields, from dinnertime until bedtime. And even then he'd stay up late—listening to talk-radio programs with urgent-sounding voices, or studying mysterious maps and diagrams he kept in fat binders. Sometimes Jory wondered if he ever slept at all.

"He'll be back before noon," Mom replied. "There's toast. Or pickles."

Jory scrunched up his face. Pickles were a running joke between him and Mom, because there were *always* pickles. Mom liked making food that kept—food that stayed good, even when shut in a cupboard for months. After this summer's harvest, the family had enough sweet pickles, stewed tomatoes, and canned pumpkin to last months and months.

"Do you need any help?" Jory asked, biting into a slice of toast.

"Sure," she replied.

He hoped she wouldn't ask for help with Ansel. Jory was still waiting for his little brother to develop a personality beyond shrieks, squeaks, and wails. Just then, he was pawing at the pencil mark Mom had made.

Jory covered it with his hand. "You're going to smudge it off," he said.

"I can always make another." Mom picked up Ansel and put him in his high chair. "Why don't you help Kit with the bread?"

"Sure." Jory dipped his finger in the flour, then tapped Kit's nose. She made claws with her floury hands and roared silently. As he reached for a wad of dough, the phone rang.

Brrrrrng.

All four of them stared at it, even Ansel. The phone *never* rang.

Finally, Mom picked up the receiver. "Hello?" She listened for a moment, then turned to Jory. "It's for you."

He blinked. "What?"

"The phone's for you. A girl—she says it's about home-work. Take it in your bedroom." She paused. "And be quick."

Jory grabbed the receiver and raced upstairs into his room. "You can't call my house!" he whispered into the phone as crossly as he could.

"Sorry," Alice said. "I just thought we could—"

"Caleb never gives out this number. Where'd you get it?"

"It was listed."

"Listed? *Where?*"

"Online!" She sounded indignant. "I just put in the name of your street. Everybody knows where you live. Who's Caleb, anyway?"

"My stepfather. Listen, you—"

"Where's your real dad?"

Jory's mouth went dry, like it always did when people asked about his father. "He's a salesman. A traveling sales-man. He travels. Look, I've got to go."

"But what about—"

He hung up. When he turned around, he saw Kit in the doorway. Her hands were still covered with flour, and she had a blob of dough on her cheek.

"Yes?" he said.

She looked at him inquiringly.

"It was nobody important," he said.

Kit put her hands on her hips, leaving dusty handprints. She peered at him until Jory sighed.

It was his own fault—he never kept secrets from Kit.

Though Kit seemed happy enough in the farmhouse and the fields, Jory did what he could to bring bits of the outside world home. He told her nearly everything that happened in class: lessons he learned, funny things the other kids did, stuff he read about during computer time. He told her the stories of *The Giver* and *Coraline*, how to determine the volume of a cube, about the Tollund Man and the Haraldskær Woman. He told her when Erik Dixon slipped on a pencil and landed on Danny Park's tuna fish sandwich—they acted it out several times, alternating who played Erik and who played the sandwich.

But for some reason, he wasn't sure how to explain Alice Brooks-Diaz. He didn't want all her questions to make Kit feel self-conscious. Jory felt self-conscious enough for the both of them.

"Just . . . this girl," he said. "From school."

Kit waited for him to go on.

"She's so nosy. Yesterday she wouldn't shut up about our house being haunted."

Kit raised her eyebrows.

"Don't worry! It's not haunted. Ghosts aren't real." Jory tried to usher Kit from his room, but she wouldn't budge. "Look," he continued, "even if they *were* real, you wouldn't have to worry about them. They're not tangible. That means you can't feel them—they can't hurt you. But it doesn't matter, because they're not real. Got it?"

She nodded.

"And even though it's never going to happen—if you wake up and there's a chalk-white face floating over your bed, punch it."

She grinned.

—

Hours later, Jory still felt annoyed. It wasn't because of Kit, though; it was because Alice had asked about his dad.

He didn't remember much about him—probably because Jory had spent so much time trying to forget. The memories had lost their color, like chalk pictures left in the rain. His dad watching noisy sports games on the television. Insisting Mom leave the house to run errands, even though she hated to. And, of course, kneeling down to say good-bye.

Jory remembered everything about Caleb, though. Especially the day they met.

After Dad left, Mom worked at a crummy coffee shop to pay for food and bills. "Crummy in a literal sense," she said. "Crumbs are *everywhere*."

She hated working there. Her back always ached and her feet always hurt. But she could handle that, she said, if it weren't for all the people. Hungry people. Shouting people. Overly caffeinated people who snapped their fingers in her face. Though the bustle didn't seem to bother the other workers, Mom said she felt like a sparrow in a flock of seagulls cawing and pecking for food.

The coffee shop's manager, a man with a shiny bald head, had no patience for Mom's anxiety. Or for Jory, even when he colored quietly at a corner table, nursing a mug of milk. Mom didn't have the money to pay a babysitter, and was far too timid to ask the neighbors in their apartment building.

Jory didn't mind, though. Especially when Mom stopped by and ruffled his hair.

"You're a regular," she told him. "The brightest part of my every day. If the manager scowls at you, ignore him."

Caleb was a regular at the coffee shop, too. Same table daily, same time. He sat alone and read hardbound books over six coffee refills, or examined binders thick with paper. Whenever he caught Jory's eye, he'd smile with his eyes.

Jory didn't know what to make of him.

Until the day Mom had one of her migraines. They arrived like swift thunderstorms, with flashing lights, stomach sickness, and pain spearing her head from temple to temple. She begged the manager to let her leave, promised she'd work overtime tomorrow.

"Not happening," he said, shaking his shiny head. He handed her a tray crowded with heavy mugs of coffee. "Take these to Table Six."

She made it halfway across the room before the crash. People screamed. Fireworks of sludgy brown coffee spiked all across the floor. The manager marched straight to Mom and hollered in her face—ignoring her coffee-splattered skin, her eyes squinched in pain.

Jory had to protect her. "Leave my mom alone!" he shrieked, throwing his crayons at the manager's legs.

The manager made a swipe for Jory's collar. "Quiet, you little—"

Suddenly, the manager toppled onto his back, sprawling in the mud puddle of coffee and broken mugs. Caleb stood over him, his eyes furious. He'd *shoved* him! Jory stared in awe.

"I'm pressing charges!" the manager shrieked. He tried to get up, but skidded onto his belly, where he flopped like a beached fish.

"You wouldn't dare," Caleb said.

He helped Mom rinse her arms in cool water. Then he drove her and Jory home to their tiny apartment. Mom's head ached so badly, she barely spoke. She climbed into bed as soon as their front door shut.

The next morning, Jory found her staring out the window.

"There's something about that man," she said.

———

Mom married Caleb a few months later, and they moved into the old farmhouse on the outskirts of town. With his soldier's pension, and by working the occasional double shift at the factory, Caleb decided Mom didn't need to work anymore. Instead, she could stay home, where she felt safe.

She would try her hand at homeschooling Jory, too. That way, they'd know exactly what he learned.

It all happened so fast, like a fairy tale.

Ever since Jory's dad had left, it was as if they'd been living in a dark, windowless room. And Caleb had led them out. He knew so much. And he'd *experienced* so much.

The first family meetings were for stories.

Like the desert snake Caleb found cooling off in his tent. "Fangs as thick as your thumbs," he said. "Eyes like marbles. A rattle like a maracas factory." He'd lured the snake to strike a hunk of wood. Then, once its fangs were stuck, he'd stomped it with both boots until it was dead, dead, dead. "Another reason boots are a man's best friend," he said.

Or the cave he'd gotten stuck inside, wedged head-to-feet between other soldiers.

Or the enemy ambush in the alley. *Stay and fight!* the superior officer had ordered. But Caleb had hidden—and the stubborn superior officer had been killed. "There's no shame in hiding," Caleb advised. "No shame in biding your time. If you're not impulsive—if you stay back and keep your eyes open—the enemy can never catch you unawares."

Caleb's whole demeanor changed as he spoke. He sat taller. His eyes sparked and flashed. His stories filled the air, snakes and storms and other enemies stalking the space behind them—but the family felt safe, always, tilting like sunflowers toward Caleb's sun.

That was when they loved him most.

But other times the war raged behind his eyes. Memories too heavy to bear. Untold stories that drove him late to bed and early to work in the mornings, leaving behind a darkness Jory could practically touch.

That was when Jory feared him.

Or not Caleb, exactly. Jory feared whatever it was Caleb had seen. What he knew.

Life with Caleb had more colors. But it also had more angles. Everything could have a hidden meaning, a different story.

Everything could be a sign.

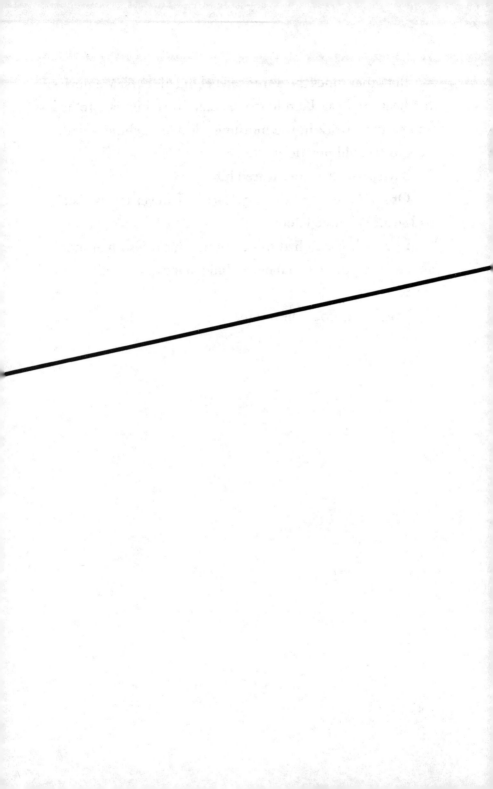

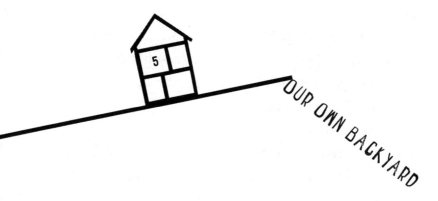

5

OUR OWN BACKYARD

THE KNOCK CAME ON SUNDAY.

The family was eating dinner: mashed potatoes and the last of the fall squash, roasted with butter. Mom had pickled the rest that morning. Just a normal evening in the old farmhouse, until—

Rap. Rap. Rap.

A blink-filled moment of silence followed. Then Caleb stood. "Probably one of those neighbor women," he muttered.

The neighbor ladies irritated Caleb, who claimed there was no such thing as being neighborly—only nosy. They'd knocked before. One time, to talk about the weather. And it was sunny out! Another time, to share a couple of jars of blueberry preserves. Caleb had accepted them grudgingly, then disposed of them as soon as the neighbor ladies left.

"We have plenty of our own preserves," he'd said. "And it's best to be wary of food from outside our family. You never know."

From the front door, Jory heard the low rumble of voices. Caleb's and a woman's—but also another man's. So it wasn't the neighbor ladies. But who could it be?

"Who's—" Jory began.

Mom shushed him.

"You're interrupting my family's dinner," Caleb said, raising his voice. "Do you have a search warrant? I didn't think so."

A search warrant? It reminded Jory of police raids he'd seen on TV, back when they had one. He remembered snarling dogs with grizzled snouts. Men in black uniforms bashing down doors. *You have the right to remain silent!*

Jory met Kit's eyes across the table. He shrugged one shoulder.

There was a longer pause. Another indecipherable rumble.

"Two," Caleb replied. "Two boys."

Before Jory could hear anything more, Mom scooped up Ansel, grabbed Kit's arm, and dragged them from the kitchen. Jory's heart pounded as he followed them into the patio.

"What's—" he began.

Mom shushed him again. It felt like forever before the front door slammed and Caleb joined them. He switched on a lantern, then settled heavily into his Adirondack chair. Mom took his hand, looking concerned.

"Who was it?" she asked.

"Officials," Caleb replied. "Sticking their noses in our family's business. I'm not sure how it happened, but we're on their radar again."

"What does that mean?"

"It means there's less time than we thought. It means—Wait, where's Kit?"

Jory discovered Kit was no longer sitting beside him. She'd drifted to the other side of the patio, where she faced the padlocked glass door, staring out.

"Kit," he called. "Come sit."

She glanced over her shoulder, then turned back to the glass.

Jory felt a flash of annoyance. Now wasn't the time to make Caleb angry. "Kit, come on!" he called.

"What's the matter with that girl?" Caleb demanded. "Has she gone deaf now, too?!"

"Maybe she's found something." Mom stood. "Honey, what is it?"

Kit didn't reply, of course. She didn't even glance their way. All of a sudden, she pivoted from the glass and scampered inside the house.

What in the world? Jory scrambled up and dashed after her, through the kitchen and into the cricket-filled evening. It was dark already, and a November chill sharpened the air.

"Kit!" he called. "Where are you going? You're going to get into trouble!"

Kit kept running. Galloping, even, her combat boots leaping soundlessly over the withered vines. Then, halfway across the pumpkin field, she stopped, her small face tipped to the sky. Her dark hair shifted in the breeze.

"What is it?" Jory panted, sliding to a stop beside her.

She pointed up.

The moon was half full and hung low over the canyon, the color of melted butter. Just above it, the navy sky was dancing. Tiny streaks of light bounced in and out of the dark.

Jory stared openmouthed. All the questions he'd had, all the worries that had jostled through his rib cage after the knock on the front door, vanished instantly. "It's the meteor shower," he said in wonder. Mr. Bradley had told them to watch for it this weekend, but he'd forgotten. Now it filled the sky, and his eyes, and his head and his heart. *So many stars.*

"Oh, how beautiful," Mom said, her voice as soft as a sigh.

She stood beside him, her honey-colored hair shining like a halo in the moonlight. Ansel was balanced on her hip, his fingers in his mouth.

Then Jory felt Caleb's hand rest on his shoulder. Not reproachfully, but protectively. A comforting weight. Together, the family watched as one by one, the stars burst into being, shot across the sky, and disappeared.

"It's a sign," Caleb said.

"A sign?" Jory asked. He and Mom looked over hopefully.

The moon shone in Caleb's eyes. "*The* sign."

The sign. *The* sign! Jory bit the insides of his cheeks. They'd been waiting for so long. He felt whooshing past him, like shooting stars, all those days and nights of searching, wondering, waiting. And now, at long last, he'd learn why. Why they'd been waiting. What they'd been waiting for.

"What does it mean?" he asked.

Caleb patted Jory's shoulder. "It means it's time to get to work. Follow me."

——

The family stood at the edge of the canyon, looking down. Despite the half moon, darkness filled it like a bottomless lake, seeping into the brush-choked canyon walls. The longer Jory stared, the less he saw.

"This is the place," Caleb said.

A slight wind ruffled through the undergrowth, and the whole canyon seemed to shudder. Jory pulled Kit closer. He felt her heartbeat vibrate through her skinny body. Or maybe it was Jory's own heart he felt.

"You see, signs aren't magical. They aren't mystical.

They have reasons behind them. If you find a dead bird, maybe there's a toxin in the air, sickening the wildlife."

"Like pollution?" Jory asked.

"Or poison," Mom added darkly.

Caleb nodded. "Exactly. If you find pages torn from a library book—or a newspaper, with the text whited out— maybe there's something the Officials don't want you to know. And a meteor shower . . . Well, it's just like I told you. Things aren't always what they seem."

A dog barked from far away, echoing in the empty space below. Jory swallowed.

"Remember what I told you about thinking for yourself? About your teachers mixing in lies with the truth? It goes for the Officials in the government, too. It goes for the whole country. The whole world. Everything is off-kilter, changing for the worse. And it's worst of all for the people at the bottom. The little people; the ordinary citizens, like us. The Officials don't tell us anything."

"That's why we have to look after ourselves," Mom added.

"That's right," Caleb said. "I've thought long and hard about how to keep the family safe in case of danger. And then it came to me." He lifted one of his big soldier's hands, sweeping it across the tangled darkness before them. "The solution was in our own backyard."

"In the canyon?" Jory asked, mystified. He'd always been told to stay out of the canyon—because of the coyotes and scorpions and big hairy spiders. Danger, capital *D*.

Caleb nodded. "In the canyon. We have lots of work to do, my family."

"All of us will help." Mom tickled Ansel's side. "Even you, baby bird."

"Almost everything we need is waiting at the bottom," Caleb said.

"Everything we need?" Jory asked.

"Everything but us."

"But . . . won't the neighbors see us?" Jory pointed at the opposite side of the canyon, where lights from a few scattered homes glowed dimly, including the neighbor ladies'. He imagined the neighbor ladies gathered around television sets, cradling bowls of popcorn and mugs of cocoa. Doing family things. Things other families did.

"They won't see us," Caleb said.

"Why not?"

Caleb took a step closer to the canyon's edge. Shadows pooled in his eye sockets. Jory thought he might be smiling, but it was hard to tell.

"Because we'll only dig at night."

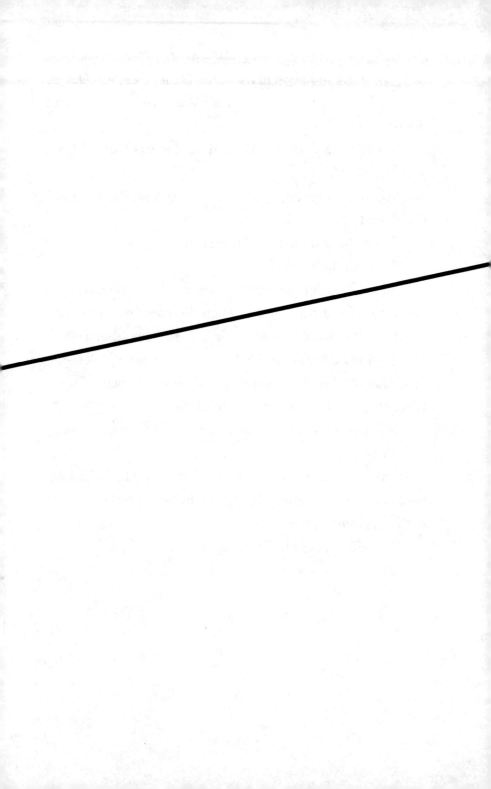

6

THE CANYON BOTTOM

AT SCHOOL ON MONDAY, the meteor shower was all anyone could talk about.

It bothered Jory. He liked to think that the falling stars had happened only for his family. But more than half his classmates had seen them.

"I can't believe I missed the meteor shower!" Alice complained at lunch, plunking herself across from Jory. "Did you remember to look?"

"I forgot, but my—" He paused. "Yeah, we saw it."

"Wow, you're so lucky. Erik tried to record it with his phone, but it was too dark . . ."

Jory rubbed his temples. He'd felt foggy-brained all morning. As if the entire weekend had been a dream—the canyon, the meteors, the visit from the Officials, Alice's phone call. Although he *did* remember hanging up on her.

But she didn't even mention it. She launched straight into the stars.

"It must have been so wild," she said. "Like the planetarium come to life! I heard it went on for like five whole minutes."

Only five minutes? It had seemed much longer than that.

She sighed dreamily. "Just think of all the wishes people made last night."

Jory smirked. Earlier, he'd overheard other boys arguing about end-of-the-world stuff. Asteroids. Hunks of fiery rock crashing into skyscrapers. Cosmic dust blotting out the sun and freezing the whole world, like in dinosaur times. Leave it to Alice to think about *wishes*.

"You're smiling," she said.

Jory straightened his face. "No I'm not."

"Well, you were! You *never* smile. Life's not all doom and gloom, Jory Birch."

Easy for Alice to say, Jory thought, as he walked home that afternoon. She wouldn't know a raincloud if it bopped her on the head. Her parents probably told her all their secrets, and never fed her pickles, and only used shovels for gardening.

Shovels. He wasn't ready to think about those yet.

Jory was so preoccupied, he walked two blocks before he realized he was on Vale Street. Uh-oh. He'd gone the short way—the wrong way.

He considered turning around. But what if somebody saw him? He could say he'd forgotten his book, *When You Reach Me*. Even though it was in his backpack.

"Jory, my man!"

Too late. Erik Dixon sat on his porch, with Sam Kapur and Randall Loomis beside him. Jory couldn't help noticing the other boys' jeans and sneakers. So comfortable-looking and normal compared to his clompy boots and cargo pants.

When Jory thought about it, dressing differently seemed like the opposite of hiding in plain sight. He was sure he'd blend in a hundred times better at school if Mom and Caleb let him swap his cargoes for jeans, low or otherwise. But he didn't ask. He knew his clothes had a purpose—even if he didn't know what the purpose was.

"We're trying to figure out how we'd spend our last day on the planet," Erik called. "If the meteors really were headed for earth. Like, inescapable annihilation. What about you?" He waved Jory over.

"What about *me*?" Jory called back, staying put.

"Yeah, man. How would you spend your last day? For example, I'd get a supersized pizza and a boat, and spend it sailing the open seas. Randall said he'd find a supermodel to make out with."

Sam elbowed Randall in the side. "Good luck finding a supermodel who'd waste her final day on earth with you. I'd break into the candy store and stuff myself."

Erik waved at Jory again. "Come over here so we don't have to yell!"

Jory didn't know what to make of Erik Dixon. He could never tell whether Erik was being genuinely friendly, or making fun of him, the way other kids sometimes did.

Sam and Randall, he was even less sure about. One time, Sam had offered to let Jory cut in the computer line. "I might take a while," he'd said. "I've got a jillion things to look up." But Jory had refused. What if Sam had wanted to look over Jory's shoulder? Even though he'd only wanted to read up on bicycle repair.

"Some other time," he called.

He was in such a hurry to get away, he walked straight into the Mendoza twins.

The twins weren't even in Mr. Bradley's class, which made their interest in Jory even more perplexing. The burly one bounced a basketball in Jory's path. "Hey, Farmer Jory!" bellowed the skinny one. "You've got hayseeds in your teeth."

"Did your tractor break down?"

"You forgot your little lamb! I thought it went every-where you go?"

Jory rolled his eyes and trudged onward. Two obstacles down. One more to go.

He braced himself as he reached the final block of Vale Street. But to his surprise, Alice's porch was empty. She must have been at her Down to Earth Club meeting—they met every Monday. Jory wasn't part of any clubs.

He watched her house a moment before walking on. Her windows had yellow curtains.

—

Caleb went first, carrying Ansel in a sling on his back. Mom went second. Kit went third, remarkably light-footed in her heavy black boots, her dark hair bound in a ponytail.

Jory went last. One step, then another and he was over the edge—inside the canyon.

Mom had woken him at midnight. Or would have woken him, if he'd ever fallen asleep. He'd tossed and turned long past his early bedtime, wondering about the night ahead.

But as soon as he'd stepped outside, the crisp night air had energized him. The shovel felt good in his hands, a perfect weight. Caleb had chosen well. He'd personalized the family's shovels: five different sizes, big to small. Even Ansel had a toddler-sized shovel, made of red plastic.

Jory used his for leverage as he navigated the canyon wall. The descent was steeper than it looked—the family's combat boots finally made sense. There were plenty of shrubs to hold on to, but Jory didn't want a poison oak surprise.

"You doing okay?" he whispered to Kit.

She glanced over her shoulder and smiled wryly. Like she found this entire late-night adventure kind of comical—and Jory supposed it was, if you squinted a bit.

At the bottom of the canyon, Caleb led them down a dark ravine, snarled with wicked-looking trees. The family's feeble flashlights only made the shadows worse. They ducked through a chaparral thicket and entered a small clearing, filled with more dirt, more brush, and more inky shadows.

But that wasn't all.

Jory saw a pair of wheelbarrows, and beside them, a hatchet. A pickax. A pair of clippers taller than Ansel, and several smaller ones. A jug of water with a spigot. Five water bottles. Folded gray tarps. Stacks of six-foot two-by-fours. And more. Even if Jory couldn't guess at each item's purpose, Caleb had thought of everything, it seemed.

"Wow!" Jory exclaimed. Then he whispered, "Sorry."

"That's all right," Caleb said. "We're free to talk here, as long as we keep our voices down. Your mother and I tested it—there's only an echo if you yell."

Jory chewed his lip. If they'd tested the echo, that meant Mom had been down here before. At the very least, she'd stood on the canyon's edge while Caleb had shouted. Jory wondered when it had happened—late at night, or when he was at school? What else did Mom know that he didn't?

"How did you get all this stuff into the canyon?" he asked.

"Some of it I carried," Caleb replied. "Some of it I brought down in the wheelbarrows. Some of it—like the wood—I drove into the main canyon and hauled from there."

Jory thought of Caleb's boots, dirt-caked in the morning. He really had been working at night. Not in the moonlit fields, but down here, in the canyon bottom. "So we're digging here?"

Caleb marched a few steps, then carved an X with his shovel. "Right here. X marks the spot."

"Are we burying something? Or digging something up? Or—or something else? I don't understand."

"Jory," Mom said sharply.

"Sorry," he said, embarrassed. He knew he was asking too many questions.

"It's okay," Caleb said. He came over and placed both hands on Jory's shoulders. "I can't tell you why we're digging yet—but it's for something very important. You'll understand soon. I promise. All I want in the world is to keep this family safe. " He looked into Jory's eyes. "Do you trust me?"

"I trust you," Jory said without thinking.

"Good." Caleb patted his shoulder, then turned to the rest of the family. Kit leaned against Mom with her arms crossed, and Ansel sat in the dirt. "Who'd like to break ground? How about Ansel?"

Ansel looked bewildered.

"That's a great idea," Mom said. She took his hand and helped him toddle to Caleb's X. "Dig right here, baby bird. You know how."

Jory felt a little envious as he watched Ansel hesitate,

then whack the ground with his plastic shovel. It barely made a dent.

"Bang!" he shouted.

"That's my boy," Caleb said, eye-beaming with pride. He hoisted his shovel. "Everybody ready?"

Overhead, the stars glittered in the blue-black sky. A night bird sang a trio of haunting notes: *low, high, low*. Unexpectedly, Jory discovered he was smiling. His eyes met Kit's, and she was smiling, too.

Sure, they didn't know *why* they were digging. But tonight, the mystery was enough.

"Do we all just dig together?" Jory asked.

"That's right," Mom said. "As a family."

7

WORLDBUILDING

FOR THE FIRST TIME SINCE HE STARTED SCHOOL AGAIN, Jory forgot to do his math homework.

"I'm sure it just slipped your mind," Mr. Bradley said, marking something in his book. "Turn it in tomorrow, and we'll be squared away."

Which was more than fair, but Jory still shriveled in his seat.

After math came social studies. "Qin Shi Huang, China's first emperor, was buried with an entire terra cotta army," Mr. Bradley began, reading from a textbook. He was so tall, sometimes his voice seemed to boom from the ceiling.

Jory leaned forward, intending to listen. He enjoyed social studies. He already had trillions of ideas for his project, mostly stuff he'd read about online during computer time: accidental mummies or Greek mythology or religious cults or folklore faeries or the Native Americans who'd inhabited the deserts east of their town.

But his mind skittered like a pebble on a slope. Last night, his family had spent four hours in the canyon. Digging, hauling dirt, picking out stones, cutting branches with pruning shears. It was almost five in the morning when Jory had shed his dirty clothes and collapsed into bed.

"Archaeologists estimate there are eight thousand terra cotta soldiers. Wow! All to protect the emperor when he woke in the afterlife."

Only two hours later, he had had to get ready for school.

"They also found one hundred and thirty chariots and six hundred and seventy horses, along with terra cotta acrobats, strongmen, and musicians. Can you imagine the thrall the emperor had over his people, to inspire them to spend years crafting his army?"

So Jory felt tired. And distracted. He had to force himself to invent some *what ifs* for Mr. Bradley's lesson. *What if the emperor had been an evil tyrant?*

What if he'd been a sorcerer?

What if his people had crafted soldiers to murder him instead of to protect him?

But Jory also felt . . . *invigorated*. Because despite the half moons of dirt beneath his fingernails, despite the ache in his weary shoulders, despite the inky blue spookiness of the canyon—it had been kind of thrilling, too.

The novelty of the night. The teamwork with his family.

And the inarguable sense that, at long last, he was getting closer to the truth. Caleb's truth. The reasons behind *everything* they did.

As the students packed up after class, Alice Brooks-Diaz tapped Jory's shoulder. She'd only ever approached him at lunch. "Jory Birch," she said. "You're smiling again."

"No I'm not," he said, smiling.

"Are too! Did you get some good news or something? A new pet?" Alice shoved back her cuffs. "Oh, *please* tell me it's a new pet. Wait—did you find a way into the locked barn? Is that why you're smiling?"

Jory shook his head and hurried away, trying and failing to straighten his face. He couldn't help it. This time, the secret wasn't being kept from him.

He was keeping the secret.

—

"I've figured out our schedules," Caleb announced.

The family was gathered in the patio for an after-school meeting. Jory sat with his back against the wall. With no shooting stars to hypnotize her, Kit knelt beside him obediently. Mom cuddled Ansel, who chewed on the end of her braid.

"Everybody's sleep schedule will be a bit different. We'll find it difficult at first, but our bodies will adapt. You'd be stunned by the schedules I kept as a soldier."

Jory attempted to look more soldierlike.

"My schedule is the only one that will vary. I'll be picking up extra shifts at the factory and running errands. Your mother will also need to run errands sometimes."

Jory glanced at Mom, who was hugging Ansel. She didn't drive, and public places overwhelmed her. Marrying Caleb meant she rarely had to leave the house, which was how she liked it. "My family's all I need," she would say. "If I only saw you guys for the rest of my life, I'd be happy as a meadowlark—or a badger, warm in its burrow."

"What kind of errands?" she asked uncertainly.

"Don't worry," Caleb replied, taking her hand. "There won't be many, I promise." He turned to Jory. "From now on, you'll have to send yourself off to school in the mornings. Your mother and the kids need more sleep than we do—we're the men of the house, after all."

Jory nodded. Beside him, Kit crossed her arms tightly.

At last, Caleb handed out the family's schedules. He'd handwritten them on beige card stock, with perfect penmanship.

JORY'S SCHEDULE
Monday to Friday:
  Dig Days.
  School 8 a.m. to 3 p.m.
  Dinner at 5 p.m.
  Sleep 6 p.m. to midnight.

> Dig midnight to 5 a.m.
> Sleep 5 a.m. to 7 a.m.
> Saturday:
> Day of Rest.
> Sunday:
> Other Preparations.
> Sleep 6 p.m. to midnight.
> Dig midnight to 5 a.m.
> Sleep 5 a.m. to 7 a.m.

Jory peered at his schedule. There was so little free time—only between three p.m. and five p.m. on weekdays. Except he'd need to finish his chores and help with dinner then, too. And when would he do his homework?

"There isn't much time to just . . ." he began, then trailed off.

"To what?" Caleb said.

Well, to play with Kit, Jory thought. But Jory knew Caleb didn't find their games important. Even if their games were important to them. "Time to relax," Jory finished.

"That's what Saturday is for," Caleb said.

"But . . ."

Caleb silenced him with a look. "Now's not the time to be selfish, Jory. This isn't about fun. This isn't a game. This is serious." He paused. "A matter of life and death."

A matter of life and death? Just this morning, Jory had been feeling excited. Now all he felt was apprehensive.

Caleb studied the family, as if assessing the impact of his words. "The harder we work now, the better off we'll be after. Just keep trusting me, and we'll be fine."

———

In the remaining twenty minutes before their new early bedtime, Jory and Kit sat cross-legged on the back porch and played Worldbuilding. It involved nailing wood scraps into the shapes of houses, then painting doors, windows, and other details with globby old paint.

Jory's houses were careful, realistic. Kit's were always peculiar, improbable: rainbow swirls, polka dots, every wall a different color. Right now, she was daubing bright orange stars on a blue rooftop. The rest of the house was green.

"Did the shooting stars hit the house?" Jory asked. "Or are the stars inside of it?"

Kit shrugged dramatically. Her palms were smudged with orange paint.

"Am I overthinking things?"

She nodded, then reached over and painted an orange star on Jory's elbow.

They'd never told Mom or Caleb about Worldbuilding. But it turned out Caleb had known all along. One day, he'd brought home a box of wood scraps and almost-empty paint cans from the factory. Perfect timing, since they'd almost run out of both.

"Just don't let your imaginations get carried away," he'd warned.

They tried not to. But over time, their Worldbuilding homes grew more elaborate: balconies, shutters, tiny two-dimensional pets, window boxes brimming with flowers—Jory's with daisy-perfect petals, Kit's bristling, neon, extra-terrestrial. They even painted little grocery stores and banks.

They only crafted towns, though. Never cities.

Mom had told them horrible stories about the city where she'd grown up. "Babies left in trash cans," she'd said. "Children kidnapped right off the streets. Everybody just walks by the homeless. You can't go ten feet without your heart breaking. It just breaks and breaks, over and over again."

"That's because you have a kind heart," Caleb had told her. Before he'd become a soldier, he'd lived in a city, too. "That's what I love about you. But you can't save everybody."

Mom had glanced at Kit. "I know that. But these people in the gutters—they're right there in front of you, asking for help. And a dollar means so much more to them than it does to you."

"Say you give one man a dollar. But what about the man around the corner?"

"One more dollar won't hurt."

"So you've given away two dollars," Caleb had said. "But are you going to give a dollar to every homeless person in the city? In the country? The whole world? Beyond? You have to draw the line someplace. Otherwise *you'll* be the one who needs to be taken care of."

He'd taken Mom's hand. "My line is a circle, around our family."

Jory had always liked that thought. A chalk line, or a force field, protecting him and his family: all five of them, safe inside. Or maybe Caleb himself was the circle, wrapping his arms around the family.

Jory and Kit never painted people in their Worldbuilding houses, though. Not their family, or anybody else's. It was kind of spooky, Jory realized now, glancing at the house in his hands. A town without residents. As if everyone had just vanished.

A matter of life and death, he thought, then swallowed it down.

He'd just dipped his brush in a cup of water when the back door creaked open. Mom leaned out. "Time for bed, my birds," she said. "We have a long night ahead of us."

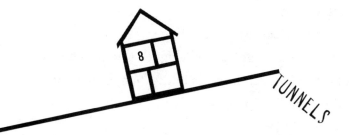

8

TUNNELS

CALEB HADN'T THOUGHT OF EVERYTHING.

Tuesday night was harder. But Wednesday night was the worst. The whole family *ached*. They stooped through the canyon like a pack of old folks. Every one of them had blisters. Even Ansel, though he didn't exactly help much.

On Thursday night, Caleb brought home a stack of heavy gloves from the factory. "Blue-collar gloves," he called them. "You could use them to throttle a porcupine."

Unlike the family's shovels, though, the gloves were all the same size. Kit's kept falling off, until Mom secured them with a rubber band.

Despite the new gloves, digging only grew more difficult. Once their shovels punched through the topsoil, the dirt was hard-packed and snarled with roots, some tiny, some thicker than Jory's arms. The worst ones snaked so deeply into the earth, he had to grab them with both hands and yank until they snapped—usually sending him flying into something thorny.

He also hadn't expected so many living things.

Not just plants, but wriggly, many-legged things. Things that skittered off his shovel onto his boots. When that happened, he had to bite his lip not to yell.

Yelling was forbidden.

Talking wasn't. But the family needed to save their breath. So it was quiet. Almost *too* quiet, Jory thought. The only sounds were the crunch of roots, the rasp of dirt sliding off their shovels, and the family's *pant-pant-pant*ing.

When they did speak, the words were muffled by the bandanas they wore to ward off the dust. Even so, it scratched their throats relentlessly, and made them rasp and cough.

Ansel spent most of the time napping in a makeshift wheelbarrow bed. Which was for the best. When awake, he quickly grew restless, and Mom or Jory would need to entertain him. Otherwise he might start plum-faced wailing, or toddle off into the ravine. Or gnaw on a rock—it had happened before.

To Jory, it would have made more sense for Kit to watch Ansel. But Caleb seemed uncomfortable leaving Kit in charge, especially in the canyon bottom. He always had an excuse. "She's too distractible tonight," he'd say. Or, "I have an important task for her right now."

Kit's size had seemed like an asset at first. She could bend into tight places and carve out stones with her tiny fingers. But she hated squeezing into the lopsided, slow-growing tunnel, infested with roots and bugs and worse. Jory could tell by her lower lip, her pinched face and bowed shoulders. Though she never protested, of course. She never even seemed to tire.

Jory *always* felt tired. He thought of his bed every time he blinked.

"One more bucketful of rocks, and then you can take a break," Caleb told him, dumping his last bucket into a wheelbarrow—quietly, so the stones wouldn't clatter.

Jory nodded. Breaks were his favorite. But they were tricky, he'd discovered. If he sat on one of the folded-up tarps for longer than a few minutes, his shoulders sagged. His head drooped. It became a monumental effort not to close his eyes, curl up, and sleep, sleep, *sleep*.

Kit never sat down, even on her breaks. She stood beside the folded tarps with her head tipped back, her eyes scanning the sky.

"Night Number Four," Jory whispered, standing next to her. "Though I guess keeping count doesn't really matter when we don't know the number we're counting to."

His throat tightened a bit at the thought. They just had to be patient, he told himself. The same way they always were. Kit shrugged one shoulder, head still tipped back.

"What are you looking at, anyway? There aren't any falling stars tonight."

She glanced at him, half-smiling. Then she reached for his hand and made him twirl her, twice, three times. When she came to a stop, she looked up again.

Jory wished he could read the sentences in her huge eyes. Sometimes he thought he knew exactly what she was thinking. Other times, like tonight, he had no clue.

"I guess you never know," he said.

—

Ever since her pumpkin-streaked arrival, Kit had been different. A *different* kind of different.

She'd slept on the floor instead of her bed. She'd eaten with her hands. Whenever anybody had tried to get her to do otherwise, she'd thrown tantrums—entirely silent. She would stand there motionless, rigid-limbed. No amount of cajoling could budge her.

Other times, she'd stare out the window for hours, though she never tried to climb out or escape. It was almost like she was waiting for someone, but no one ever came.

Mom thought she needed special help. "They have counselors at the elementary school," she'd suggested. "Maybe they can help her."

"Not if you want to keep her," Caleb had warned. "They'll inform the Officials. And the Officials might take her away."

Take her away.

No wonder they had to keep Kit a secret.

Jory never knew if she'd overheard that conversation. But after that, Kit began to mind. She slept in her bed, and ate with a knife and fork like she'd known how to the whole time. She helped Mom in the kitchen. She read every book Mom gave her, and all of Jory's, too.

"How do you know she's not just staring at the pages?" Caleb asked one evening, after Kit was in bed. "If she can't tell you what she's read, or write essays about it?"

"She nods and shakes her head," Mom replied. "When I ask her yes or no questions, she gets every answer right."

"Then why doesn't she write? Or speak, for that matter?"

Mom didn't know.

"So it's stubbornness," Caleb said. "Or spite."

Mom shook her head adamantly. "She's a good girl. Only confused. It's almost like . . . she speaks another language." She looked thoughtful. "Or doesn't remember how to speak ours."

Caleb sat there, scratching his beard.

To him, Kit was serious, even dull. Mom called her solemn, and worried about her fading spirit.

But Mom didn't need to worry. With Jory, Kit was downright feisty. A hands-on-her-hips kind of girl, who stuck out her tongue and rolled her eyes as soon as backs were turned. A lively, creative girl, who skipped alongside him in the fields, leaped over grabby-fingered vines, twirled and spun majestically in her tattered ballet shoes. Who painted their wooden houses improbable colors. Who stalked blackbirds within a couple of feet—and they'd just *stare* at her, beady-eyed and unafraid, until she flapped her skinny arms and sent them soaring.

Kit's spirit hadn't left her. She saved it for Jory.

Sometimes Jory wanted to take her hand and lead her into town. A girl who sparked so bright shouldn't be confined to the farmhouse and the fields. But Jory never forgot what Caleb had said, way back at the beginning.

The family had to keep Kit safe—which meant keeping her secret.

Or else, the Officials might take her away.

—

By the second week, Jory was bringing the canyon to school.

Scribbles of branches lurked behind his eyelids. Every time he inhaled, he breathed the musty-sagey smell of canyon bottom. His pencil felt tiny and foreign in his fingers, because it wasn't a shovel.

He forgot Monday's homework on Wednesday. He also forgot Tuesday's—and Wednesday's, and Thursday's. The X by his name quadrupled into an angry red forest. *I'll make up all of it over the weekend,* he'd promised himself.

But he didn't.

It was so stupid. He'd spent so much time trying to blend

into the backdrop at school. Avoiding anything that might make him stand out, even raising his hand. But every day that week, the whole class had stared as Mr. Bradley marked his book. Jory had never felt more embarrassed in his—

"Mr. Birch?"

"What?" Jory said. It came out snappy, not like he'd meant it.

Mr. Bradley paused. A nervous giggle tittered through the class.

"I asked," Mr. Bradley said quietly, "if you'd decided on a topic for your social studies project."

"Sorry. My topic is, um . . ." Jory dug through his brain. Last week, he'd thought of so many ideas—he knew he had. But he couldn't unearth a single one in the confusion of roots and dirt.

"Yes?"

The class was staring. Jory felt frantic. All he could think of was canyons and darkness and shovels and digging . . .

"If you need help—"

"Tunnels," he said.

He tried not to cringe. What kind of a topic was *tunnels*? One too close to home, that was for sure.

Mr. Bradley stopped Jory on his way to lunch. "Can we talk for a sec?"

Jory nodded, fighting the heat in his cheeks. "What is it, sir?"

"Sir!" Mr. Bradley's inch-long dimples appeared. "I

haven't been called that in a long time. I wanted to hear a little more about your project. Where did you get the idea?"

"I . . ." Jory thought fast. "It was that Chinese emperor you were talking about. With the armies buried underground. I just thought—well, tunnels. There must have been lots of tunnels." Good save, he thought.

"Ah," Mr. Bradley said.

"But I'm interested in other kinds of tunnels, too," Jory added. "All kinds."

"Well, I look forward to reading about them! Especially after your essay on venomous animals. You always ask questions I would never have thought of. In fact, your papers get *me* thinking."

"Really?"

Mr. Bradley nodded. "Really."

"Wow." Jory grinned, feeling warm all over. Here, he'd thought he was in trouble, when Mr. Bradley just wanted to compliment him. His paper on venomous animals *had* been pretty great, particularly the part about spitting cobras.

"You can see why I'm concerned about all that missed homework," Mr. Bradley went on.

Uh-oh.

"Is everything okay? Anything you want to talk about?"

"Yes, of course," Jory said quickly. "I mean, no, there's nothing. Nothing to talk about."

"Nothing I should be concerned about?"

"Nope! Everything's just fine." Jory had to force a grin

this time. "I'll catch up, I promise. Can I go to lunch now? I'm really hungry." He wished could make his stomach growl on command. Even better, he wished he had a tunnel he could crawl inside.

Mr. Bradley sighed. "All right, Jory. Go ahead."

Jory hurried for the door.

"Hey, Jory?"

He glanced over his shoulder. "Yes?"

"You're a smart guy," Mr. Bradley said. "Why don't you raise your hand from time to time?"

"I . . ." Jory shrugged. "Yeah, okay. I'll try."

As soon as he stepped outside, he shoved his hands in his pockets.

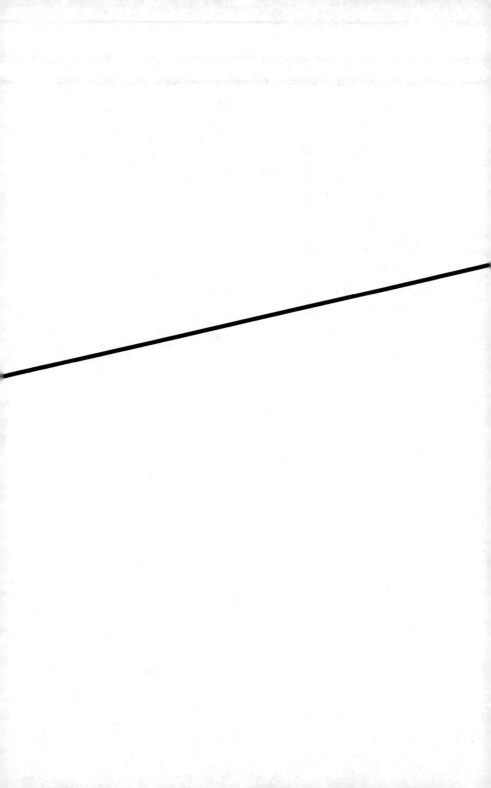

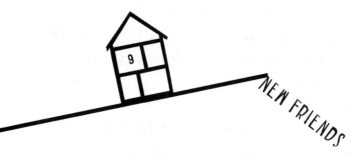

9

NEW FRIENDS

A SIREN HOWLED THROUGH JORY'S DREAMS. He jerked up in bed, confused and groggy. It wasn't even dark yet—he'd only been asleep twenty minutes, tops. Sleeping before sundown still felt wrong.

Brrrrrng. Brrrrrng.

It wasn't a siren—it was the telephone.

Oh no. What if Alice was calling again? Jory had warned her not to, but . . .

He threw back his covers and slipped into the hall. Kit already stood at the top of the stairs, swaddled in her flowered blanket, listening. Or appearing to listen. There's no way she can hear what they're saying, Jory thought. The kitchen was too far away.

Suddenly, Kit rushed down the hall toward her room. Jory blinked a moment, then hustled to his. Half a minute after he dived under the covers, someone knocked on his door.

"Family meeting," Caleb said, leaning in. "Right now."

The patio glowed pink in the light of the sunset. Jory was too worried to sit, but too sleepy to stand. He leaned against a wall, arms crossed.

"Who called?" Mom asked, her arms around Ansel.

"Tom Bradley," Caleb said. "Jory's teacher."

Instantly, Jory was wide awake. This was worse than Alice. So much worse.

"He claims you haven't been acting like yourself in class. That you've seemed tired. And that you've missed a whole week of homework assignments."

Jory's stomach seemed to topple into the canyon. He never imagined Mr. Bradley would call his house. Home was home and school was school.

"I understand the family's new schedule has been challenging," Caleb said, his intense eyes locked on Jory. "I thought we'd adjust after a few days, but apparently that hasn't been the case for all of us."

"I'll try harder," Jory said. "I know I'll get used to it. . . ."

"Jory's the only one in school," Mom said softly. "It can't be easy for him."

Caleb sighed.

"Maybe it's time to homeschool him again?" Mom suggested. "Ansel's older now, and less trouble. Kit can watch him while I take care of Jory's lessons."

Jory felt an odd hitch in his middle. His feelings about school were complicated, but he didn't want to *leave* it.

"I don't think so," Caleb said.

"It'll be no trouble—"

"It's not a good idea. Pulling him out of school will focus more attention on our family. Especially since this Tom Bradley already has his eye on us." Caleb looked out the window. "We need all the time we can get. Because we don't have that much time left."

A chill crawled down Jory's spine.

"Then what can we do?" Mom asked.

"From now on, Jory will take Tuesdays off from digging," Caleb said. "The rest of the family can go to bed at three p.m., but we'll still work in the canyon on Tuesday night. Jory, will that be enough time for you to catch up?"

Jory nodded. "Yes, sir."

Inside, he was shriveling. When Caleb was proud of him, he called him son. When he was disappointed, he called him Jory.

"Now that we've all gathered here, how about a story?" Caleb said.

He reached for Ansel, and Mom passed him over. Ansel didn't look as comfortable with Caleb as with Mom, Jory thought, but at least he didn't cry.

Caleb switched on a lantern. Then he began.

As always, he set the scene so vividly, Jory could feel it. The desert alley bullied by a heavy sun. Dust everywhere.

Too much to carry. A team led by a superior officer who told them little.

"The less soldiers know," Caleb explained, "the easier it is for them to follow orders. Innocence encourages trust. And trust breeds obedience."

The family had heard this story many times before. The pounding boots. The soldiers' yells. The *clap bang rat-a-tat-tat* of the artillery echoing through the alley. When Caleb was in a good mood, he'd mimic the noises, tickling Ansel on his lap. The story seemed almost lighthearted—well, optimistic, anyway. A parable about how smart Caleb was, thinking for himself.

Tonight, though, Jory smelled the gunpowder. The bitter tang of smoke. The terror gripping the soldiers when the superior officer ordered them to *Charge!*

"In that moment," Caleb said, "I had a choice. I could stay and fight, like my superior officer ordered—and face certain death. Or I could defy orders and save my own life."

Jory knew what came next, but he still held his breath.

"I stepped into the shell of a burnt-out building. Then came a blast so loud my hearing blanked out. I waited. And waited. When I was certain of the silence, I went out to investigate. Everybody had been killed. All my fellow soldiers—and my superior officer, too.

"I was alive—I *am* alive—because I listened to my instincts. Because I trusted myself."

This was when Caleb usually looked at each family

member, one by one. But this time, he only looked at Jory.

"Only follow orders from people you trust," he said. "Do you trust me?"

"Of course," Jory said.

"Then remember. There's no shame in staying back and keeping your eyes open. There's no shame in hiding."

—

The next morning, as Jory was about to leave for school, he discovered a square of card stock taped to the front door.

JORY'S NEW SCHEDULE
Monday:
    Dig Day.
    School 8 a.m. to 3 p.m.
    Dinner at 5 p.m.
    Sleep 6 p.m. to midnight.
    Dig midnight to 5 a.m.
    Sleep 5 a.m. to 7 a.m.
**Tuesday:
    Jory's night off.**
Wednesday to Friday:
    See Monday.
Saturday:
    Day of Rest.

Sunday:
Other Preparations.
Sleep 6 p.m. to midnight.
Dig midnight to 5 a.m.
Sleep 5 a.m. to 7 a.m.

Jory frowned, then shoved it into his pocket.

In class, he tried his best not to slouch. Or yawn. Or do anything that might inspire Mr. Bradley to glance his way. Whenever he caught his mind drifting, he pinched his leg under the table and remembered he'd get *plenty* of sleep that night.

Eight full hours. Or more, even. If he wanted—after homework, of course—he could go to sleep after dinner and not wake until morning. He'd never felt more excited about his bed.

But first, he had to get through the rest of the school day.

All day long, he noticed Mr. Bradley watching him. Jory had no idea why, especially since he'd managed to complete yesterday's homework on time.

He didn't figure it out until science.

Mr. Bradley was discussing hydrothermal vents: big fissures in the earth that brought warmth and life to the deepest parts of the ocean. "Entire ecosystems thrive around these vents," Mr. Bradley said. "They're like underwater desert oases. Hundreds of new deep-sea creatures have been discovered in otherwise barren places."

"It's freaky to think about what's down there," said Paisley Matthews with a shudder.

"*Fascinating*, you mean!" exclaimed Alice.

"Remember to raise your hand, girls," Mr. Bradley said. "So how do scientists explore the deep sea, anyway? Anybody know?"

Danny Park raised his hand, and Mr. Bradley called on him. "Probably submarines," Danny said.

"Right. Special submarines. But why are submarines necessary? Why can't scientists strap on a dive tank and see for themselves?"

Alice raised her hand. "It'd take too long," she said. "They wouldn't have enough oxygen to make it there and back."

Mr. Bradley nodded. "It takes a lot of time to dive safely. Any other reasons?"

Jory's fingers twitched. He'd just read about scuba diving online! All of a sudden, he realized the best way to hide in plain sight. Before he could chicken out, he did something he'd never done before.

He raised his hand.

Mr. Bradley beamed. "Yes, Jory?"

"Because—" Jory cleared his throat and tried again. "Because of the pressure. All that water creates pressure.

Enough to crush any diver, even if they could bring down enough air to get there."

"If a giant squid doesn't crush you first!" added Erik Dixon.

Jory glanced at him, but Erik's smile wasn't mocking.

"Very good, Jory," said Mr. Bradley. "And it's true, giant squids do live deep in the ocean. Along with all kinds of other creatures, like beaked whales and spider crabs. Many others are still a mystery, since that kind of depth and darkness is so difficult to explore."

"Probably a good thing," Erik said. "If everything down there's so dangerous."

"Not all deep-sea creatures are dangerous, of course," said Mr. Bradley. "Not *every* mystery is a danger. Right, Alice?"

"Right," Alice said with a grin.

Jory clasped his hands under his desk as the discussion continued around him. It hadn't been so bad, speaking up in class. Everyone had looked at him, just like he'd feared.

But then they'd looked away.

—

As Jory walked home after school, he wondered if the family was asleep already, gathering strength for the night ahead. The family, minus Jory. A strange thought. Would they miss him?

"Hey, it's Farmer Jory!"

Jory halted, eyes wide. He was on Vale Street. He swiveled all the way around before he was certain—because seriously, *again?* At least Erik Dixon hadn't been sitting on his porch. But Erik was small potatoes compared to the Mendoza twins.

"What's in all those pockets?" taunted the skinny one.

"I'll bet it's piglets. Piglets and baby chicks."

"That's not very nice, Farmer Jory. They might suffocate in there."

The basketball hit Jory in the knee this time. He made fists in his pockets. Not that he knew how to use them, if he ever attempted a punch. He'd probably miss and hit a tree.

"Jory Birch!"

That wasn't a Mendoza—it was Alice Brooks-Diaz, jogging up beside them.

The twins grinned when they saw her. "Hi Alice," the skinny one said.

"Nice buns," the burly one said, waggling his eyebrows.

"You twins are bimbos," Alice said. "You're human waste. I'm ashamed to share oxygen with you. Let's go, Jory."

Part of Jory wanted to march right past her. Who did she think she was, sticking her baby koala face in his business? Luckily, the rest of him realized he was being stupid.

As they walked down Vale Street, Alice rambled about those idiot Mendoza twins, the untrustworthiness of her double-crossing friend Paisley Matthews, and the supposed location of Mr. Bradley's secret tattoo. Some kids claimed he had a rattlesnake on his bicep. Erik Dixon swore it was the face of the musician David Bowie, whom Jory had never heard of. He didn't want to say so, though.

"I'd never get a tattoo I didn't draw myself," Alice said. "Like an octopus. Those are my favorite. Did you know they're incredibly intelligent? I saw a video of one unscrewing a jar from the inside! It'd be hard to draw all those legs, though. Maybe I should go for something more reasonable, like a cat with a teeny tiny hat on . . ."

At long last, they reached Alice's house.

"Here's my house," she said, as if Jory didn't know already. "For now, anyway. When they finish the new housing development on the edge of town, we're going to move there. I'm not sure how I feel about that. Old houses have more character, don't you think?"

"I guess," Jory said. "Well . . . it was nice talking with you."

"Talking with me?" She rolled her eyes. "You haven't said a thing. You hardly ever do."

He wondered why she was pointing it out after all this time. "I just did."

"You are one exasperating person, Jory Birch. Did you know that? You're lucky I don't have a frying pan to bonk you with. Also, you're different."

Jory shrugged. "Not like that's anything new."

"I mean like, *weirdly* different. Even for you. You're all slopey-looking."

"What does that even mean?"

"You know. Slopey." She drooped her shoulders, dangling her arms like an ape.

"I don't look like that!" he said indignantly. "I'm only tired, is all. I . . . I have a lot of chores."

"Farm chores?"

"What? No, not farm chores. Why does everyone think I live on a farm?"

"Well, technically, you do. Right?"

"No! I mean, maybe it used to be one. But not anymore. Real farms have, like, chickens. And geese."

"I'd like a pet goose," Alice said. "Once I read that you can keep them as attack dogs. Attack geese! Imagine if I visited your farm, and this attack goose came barreling toward me, all crazy honking and flapping and—do geese have teeth?"

"We don't have any geese."

"Are you sure?" She lowered her voice. "Maybe they're in the locked barn."

Jory stared at her in bewilderment. Then he realized she was kidding. "Very funny. I've really got to go. I have to work on my social studies project."

"Why don't you work on it here?"

He stared at her. Linked like that, those seven familiar words became entirely foreign. Nobody had ever asked him to come over.

"Don't look at me like that!" Alice exclaimed.

"Like what?"

"All startled and owlish and circle-eyed. It's not like I asked you to steal a convertible."

"A convertible?"

Alice sighed gustily. "I just figured you don't have a computer at home, all right? I mean, why else would a person handwrite all his essays?"

"Thanks," Jory said. "But really, it's all right. I don't need a computer. I have lots of books."

"Books about tunnels?"

"Your parents don't know me."

"Oh my gosh, Jory. Stop making everything into such a big deal! My parents love it when I bring new friends over."

He felt a tug in the center of his chest. *New friends.*

When he thought about it, he couldn't see anything wrong with stopping by, just for a little bit. Especially since Caleb was at work, and Mom, Kit, and Ansel were already asleep.

It's not like he was stealing a convertible, after all.

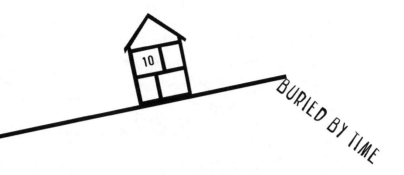

BURIED BY TIME

"So who's this?" asked Mrs. Brooks-Diaz.

It was pretty innocent, as questions went, but it still made Jory want to turn and run. He hoped he didn't look too slopey. Or owlish.

"It's Jory Birch," Alice said. "He's in my class. He lives on a farm."

Mrs. Brooks-Diaz smiled at him. She was much taller than Mom—half a foot, even—and wore a bun like Alice's, but only one. Her skin was darker than her daughter's. "A farm? Is that right?"

"Not exactly." Jory shot a glare at Alice, who grinned.

"Well, it's nice to meet you, either way." Mrs. Brooks-Diaz offered her hand. "I'm Mrs. Brooks."

He looked at her quizzically. "Not Brooks-Diaz?"

"I'm Mrs. Brooks," she said again, "and my husband's

Mr. Diaz. We decided to keep our last names when we got married. Alice is half each of us, so she gets to share both names."

"That's very sweet, Mom," Alice said. "So listen, Jory here needs to use our computer. His family's isn't working. If, y'know, you feel like dropping off any snacks, we'll be in the office."

"Why didn't you tell her the truth?" Jory asked quietly as Alice led him upstairs.

"About what, your computer?" Alice shrugged. "I didn't want to embarrass you."

"I'm not embarrassed," he said, embarrassed. "I'm just surprised you lie to your mom."

"Well, it's not like I lie about anything serious or hazardous or whatever—I always tell the truth when it matters. But in this case, she didn't *need* to know. So I made something up."

Jory supposed that made sense.

Although he couldn't imagine lying to Mom. Or to Caleb. Even if it wasn't about anything serious or hazardous or whatever, it would be too disrespectful. No, worse: a betrayal.

And besides—Caleb would *know*.

He sat at the desk Alice motioned to, in a chair that made it impossible to slouch. She called it *ergonomic*. "My dad has a slipped disk," she explained, settling into an armchair with her family's laptop.

Jory saw his face reflected in the dark computer screen. I do look sort of owlish, he thought, before waking the mouse. He knew he needed to hurry—he didn't want to overstay his welcome. Like the neighbor ladies, who thought discussing blue jays and weather forecasts were acceptable reasons to interrupt the family's Sunday lunch.

He opened a browser window and typed "tunnels" into the search engine.

Then he deleted it and typed "signs."

Then he deleted it and typed "tunnels throughout history."

———

Tunnels were everywhere.

Fox dens. Ant colonies. Manmade tunnels—and more. *Tons* of important things were underground. Basements. Bunkers. Bomb shelters. Sewer systems. Subways.

There were even entire underground cities in places like Seattle and Jerusalem. Though they hadn't started out underground—they'd been buried by time.

But in Jordan, there was an ancient city called Petra carved into the side of a cliff. Not just homes, but also tombs and temples and monasteries. And there were cliff-side Native American villages, too, in wild western places like Colorado and Wyoming. They weren't entirely underground, but partially.

He read about morgues and mausoleums. Rappelling and spelunking.

He read about Qin Shi Huang, the Chinese emperor Mr. Bradley had told them about, and his terra cotta army. He read about Pompeii in Italy and Joya de Cerén in El Salvador, both ancient cities buried by volcanic ash. In Joya de Cerén, the people had escaped. In Pompeii, most of them hadn't.

He read about so many things, and for so long, that when Alice spoke he nearly hit the ceiling. "Are you staying for dinner?" she asked.

"Um," Jory said, trying to compose himself. "Sorry. I just—what time is it?"

"It's almost six. We're eating in half an hour. Dad's making turkey burgers. With avocado."

Almost six? He'd been sitting at the computer for *two hours*. His face felt hot. Why hadn't Alice said anything?

"He can leave off the avocado, if you—"

"It's—my family's waiting for me," Jory said. Which wasn't true, obviously. But he'd never stayed out this late before, and for some reason, that alarmed him. Plus, Caleb always said to be wary of food other than their family's. "They're making . . ." Pickles. The only food he could think of was pickles. "But thanks for the . . . for the Internet."

"Sure," Alice said, following him to the door. "Any time. And if you ever feel like staying for dinner, my dad's a really good cook. Well, except for the time he tried to make chimichangas. Did you know those aren't even really Mexican? Mom called it an insult to his heritage . . ."

Jory hurried out.

As he crossed the bridge, the black-and-white dog appeared, almost like magic. Its pink tongue lolled sideways out of its mouth. Its nose was the color of cinnamon.

"Get lost," Jory said.

The dog didn't get lost. It trotted alongside him.

"You should go to Alice Brooks-Diaz's house," Jory told it. "Maybe she'll give you a turkey burger. With or without avocado."

But the goofy-faced dog followed him all the way home. Like it had no place to be, no place to go.

What if the dog was a sign? Would Caleb let them keep it? Kit would love it—animals delighted her, like the gray fox she'd once frolicked after in the fields. Ansel, Jory was less sure about. Once a wild rabbit had hopped too close, and he'd started to wail.

Jory paused outside the back door. "Stay," he ordered the dog.

He headed for the kitchen and opened the fridge. A plate of spaghetti squash sat front and center. There was a note, too, half-soaked in red tomato sauce.

For your supper
Love, Mom

Jory smiled at it, then set it aside. Food in jars filled the rest of the fridge. Same with the cupboards, along with food in cans and pouches. *What would a dog like?* he wondered. Pickled peppers? Pickled pickles? Tuna, maybe?

He decided on a pouch of tuna, a slice of bread, and an uncooked potato. But when he brought them to the back door, the dog was gone.

———

By eight in the evening, Jory's eyelids felt like heavy stones. His writing hand felt like a shovel. He fell asleep on last Tuesday's math homework, and again on last Thursday's. Finally, he climbed into bed, promising himself he'd get up in an hour and finish the rest.

A few hours later, a heavy *thunk* woke him. It sounded like it was coming from outside. He listened, but didn't hear it again. Probably a raccoon, he thought, or a disgruntled opossum.

As soon as he lay back again, Kit threw open his door.

She wore her combat boots, a hooded sweatshirt, and her usual cargo pants. She bounded across the room and pounced on Jory's bed, poking and prodding him to get up.

"I'm not going to the canyon tonight," he mumbled.

Kit continued to prod him playfully, like she thought he was joking.

"Quit it!" Jory pushed her away. "I've got Tuesdays off now. Remember?"

She stared at him blankly.

"You were *there*, Kit. It was Caleb's decision, not mine."

Her eyes narrowed. She slid off the bed and backed away a step.

"It's just once a week." Jory started to feel unsettled. "I'm sorry. I'll be there with you tomorrow. You'll be fine one night without me—just one night a week, all right? Kit?"

Kit's scowl only deepened, darkened, like a storm was brewing behind her face. Her cheeks bloomed angry pink. Finally, she swiveled on her boot heel and marched out of Jory's room, slamming the door behind her.

Jory stared at the closed door, feeling regretful. Then guilty.

Then annoyed.

Sure, it was nice having an extra night off. But it wasn't Jory's fault he had so much homework. *She* should try going to school for a change, and dealing with human waste like the Mendoza twins on way too little sleep.

He punched his pillow into shape and rolled over. But he had trouble closing his eyes.

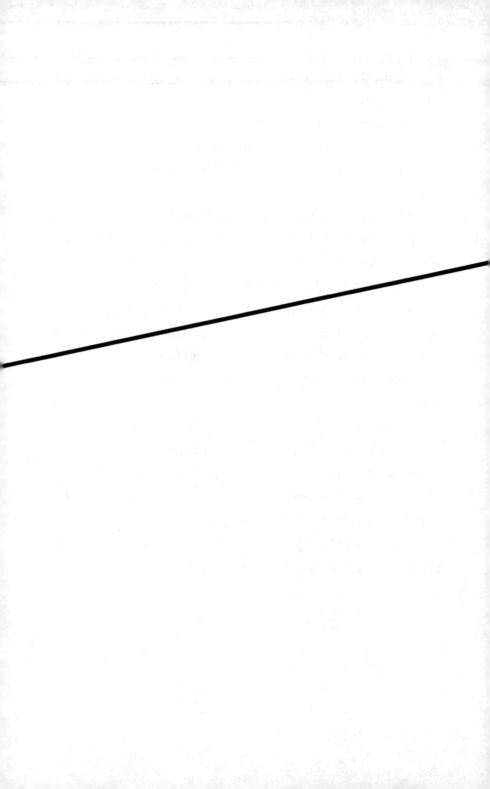

MADE OF STARS

THE MENDOZA TWINS NEVER APPROACHED JORY at school. In fact, Jory rarely saw them, since they were in a different sixth grade class.

But on Wednesday, they seemed to be everywhere. Glaring in the hallway. Frowning in the schoolyard. Glowering in the cafeteria when Alice Brooks-Diaz sat across from him.

"How's the tunnel project coming?" she asked, peeling a banana.

"I've only just started it," he replied, glancing over her shoulder at the Mendoza twins. "You were there."

"I know. But maybe you came up with some good ideas last night."

"Last night I was sleeping."

"So what? I do most of my thinking while I'm asleep."

Alice speared a slice of banana with a plastic fork, then looked at Jory expectantly.

"What?"

"This is when you ask me how *my* project is coming."

"Sorry. How's your project coming?" He hesitated. "Wait, what *is* your project?"

"Space exploration," she said. "It's going just fine, thank you for asking. Although I think it's giving me an existential crisis."

"A *what*?"

"Have you ever just laid there in the dark, and thought about stuff like—I don't know, life and death and time and space? Outer space? How big and endless it all is? And then suddenly you have to wiggle your toes and pinch your cheeks to make sure you still exist? That's an existential crisis."

"I'm not sure," Jory said.

"Oh. Well, anyway, I'm learning lots of interesting stuff. Like did you know that ninety-three percent of people are made of stardust?"

"Really?" He considered it. "So . . . only seven percent of people aren't?"

"No—I mean *everybody*," Alice said, laughing. "Ninety-three percent of everyone's body is made of stardust. Of elements that came from stars, specifically. From before the earth even existed."

"Huh," Jory said.

Alice beamed. "Isn't it amazing? We're both made of stars, Jory Birch. Everybody is."

———

By the time school ended, Jory had forgotten about the Mendoza twins. Until they called his name.

"Hey, Farmer Jory!"

Jory double-checked a street sign to make sure he'd chosen the long way. He had—which meant the twins had followed him.

This wasn't good.

The skinny one caught up to him first. He slung a bony arm over Jory's shoulder. "Why'd you have to embarrass us in front of Alice like that?"

"I don't—what?" Jory felt utterly baffled. "When?"

"After school yesterday."

He thought back. "I don't even think I said anything."

"You know what you did."

The burly one leaned in Jory's face. His breath smelled like lunch meat. "I could snap you like a stick insect, Farmer Jory."

"Like a *stick*, you mean?"

"You think you're so smart, you twerpy little hick."

Twerpy little hick? Jory sighed. Even though he'd gotten plenty of sleep last night, he still felt tired. Mr. Bradley had accepted Jory's stack of belated homework with a smile.

But when he learned Jory had fallen asleep on last night's assignment, he'd frowned. "Don't you think you should have completed last night's first?" Which made sense. But so did Jory's way.

Anyway, he was tired. "Don't you guys have anything better to do?" Jory asked the twins. "I've got to get home. My family's waiting for me."

"You mean, your family of weirdo farmer freaks?"

Suddenly, Jory woke up. He could handle the twins insulting him, but not his family. "*What* did you say?"

"I said, go chew some hay with your freaky farmer family," the burly one said. "Go milk a bull."

"A *cow*, you mean?"

"You think you're so smart," the burly one said again.

"*I think I'm so smart*," Jory repeated, ducking out from under the skinny one's arm. "You know what? I *am* smart. Compared to you two idiots, anyway."

The twins stared at him, slack-jawed.

"I'll kick your—" the burly one began.

Before he could finish, Jory was halfway down the block. He could hear the twins hollering behind him. They were chasing him. And they were *catching up*. This was turning out to be a terrible idea.

He needed a new one.

Quickly, Jory recalled Caleb's story—the one where the superior officer had ordered the soldiers to stay and fight.

There's no shame in hiding.

Jory sprinted around the corner, eyes darting. A playhouse—too obvious. A mailbox—too small. A juniper hedge—scratchy, and also probably spider-infested.

A doghouse—just right.

He checked to make sure there was no rottweiler. Then he dove inside. He curled up with his arms around his knees, his chin in the cleft between them. The space was dark and reeked like dog, which made Jory think of the black-and-white one.

He liked that dog, to be honest. He wished he could choose the moments it barked into his life. Like right now. Except it'd also need to be big enough to eat the Mendoza twins' faces.

Then he heard a commotion just outside the doghouse. Shoes slapped the pavement. "Farmer Jory!" the skinny one called. "Come on, we just want to talk!"

"Where'd he go?" asked the burly one as they panted past.

"I don't know! That dumb hick vanished into thin air . . ."

Jory counted to twenty. Then he crawled out of the doghouse on all fours, scraping his forehead in the process. It hurt. Still, he couldn't help grinning. Hiding had worked! Caleb might not tell Jory much, but he told him what was important.

Well, except where digging was concerned.

—

That night, the stars shone through wispy clouds. The moon was yellow. A harvest moon, Mom called it. It signaled the ripening of crops, the perfect time to pick, although they'd already harvested everything in the fields. Chopped it and boiled it and pickled it in mason jars.

As Jory hiked through the chaparral thicket, he wondered what progress his family had made without him.

Not much, it turned out. The heap of brush-covered dirt didn't look any larger. The hole—a crooked gash, really, like a smirk in the earth—looked exactly the same size. Jory figured he'd have to stay away a week to see any difference. It was a lot like growing. You didn't notice unless you made marks on the doorjamb, the way Mom did, measuring their height months apart.

But Jory knew he'd never get a weeklong vacation. Night after night, he'd be down here in the canyon bottom.

How many nights until they finished?

It depended, of course, on what they were digging for. For a moment, Jory let himself wonder. People dug for lots of reasons, the Internet had informed him. They dug to make things. They dug to find things. They dug to hide things. He hadn't read about families digging tunnels in their own backyards, though. Maybe he'd look it up on Alice's computer next time.

If there was a next time.

Alice had seemed open to the possibility, anyway. She'd even asked Jory to dinner. He'd never had a turkey burger.

He liked turkey all right, although he didn't care much for avocado. He'd have to ask for his burger without—that is, if he could trust her family's food.

Of course he could. That was silly. Alice ate her family's food every day, and she seemed perfectly healthy.

"You all right?" Caleb asked Jory, making him jump.

"Yes, sir," he said quickly. He stood up straighter. "I'm doing just fine."

"Good. I hope you're feeling well-rested—we've got lots of work to do." Caleb paused, resting a hand on Jory's shoulder. "Want to tell me what happened to your forehead?"

Jory winced. He wondered whether he should make something up, like Alice had with her parents. Then he felt ashamed for even considering it. He couldn't lie to Caleb.

"It was a doghouse," he said.

"A doghouse?"

"I was hiding in it." Jory had felt clever at the time—even brave. Now he just felt stupid. "There are these two guys . . . the Mendoza twins. They're in my grade, but much bigger than me. Anyway, they were—well, I thought of your story, about the superior officer and the ambush in the alley."

"You did?"

Jory nodded. "Instead of fighting, I hid in a doghouse. I stayed back and kept my eyes open. Just like you said I should."

"Sounds like you made the right decision." Caleb patted Jory's shoulder. "I'm proud of you, son."

Jory's heart swelled in his chest. "Thank you," he said.

Caleb lifted up his shovel. "Would you mind asking Kit to sort stones?"

Kit was standing just a few yards away. But Caleb avoided speaking to her directly. "Just the way fathers are with daughters," Mom had told Jory. "Ages ago, mine was the same way."

Jory found Kit using a stick to pry a dirt clod from her boot. "Caleb wants you to sort rocks. Better than digging, at least."

She glanced at him. Then she hurled the stick with all her might. It arced high into the sky, higher than seemed possible when flung by such a skinny arm, before falling into a far-off patch of brush.

"Are you all right?" Jory asked.

Kit just turned and walked away. She couldn't still be angry after last night, could she? He hadn't even *done* anything.

And yet it bothered him all night, like an itch he couldn't reach.

———

In his dreams that night, Jory stood outside Kit's bedroom. The doorknob felt like ice. He knew he had to enter, but he was frightened.

Not for Kit—but *of* Kit.

Which made no sense, so he opened the door.

His sister stood at the window, looking out. Her face was bathed in blue-gray moonlight. Her black hair fluttered and shifted, as if caught in a breeze. But the window was closed. He couldn't tell what she was looking at, but she was riveted.

"What is it?" Jory asked.

"It's so beautiful," Kit replied.

After three years of silence, her voice seemed to echo, dancing inside Jory's chest and head. Like an old song he'd loved, but couldn't remember. Like a dream he'd forgotten, but couldn't forget.

"What's so beautiful, Kit?"

She didn't answer. The breeze picked up, until it became a wind, until her hair flew like a black banner behind her. Jory couldn't tell if the room had grown cold or hot.

"What's so beautiful?" He felt frantic. "What is it?"

At last, Kit turned to Jory.

Her eyes were shaped like stars.

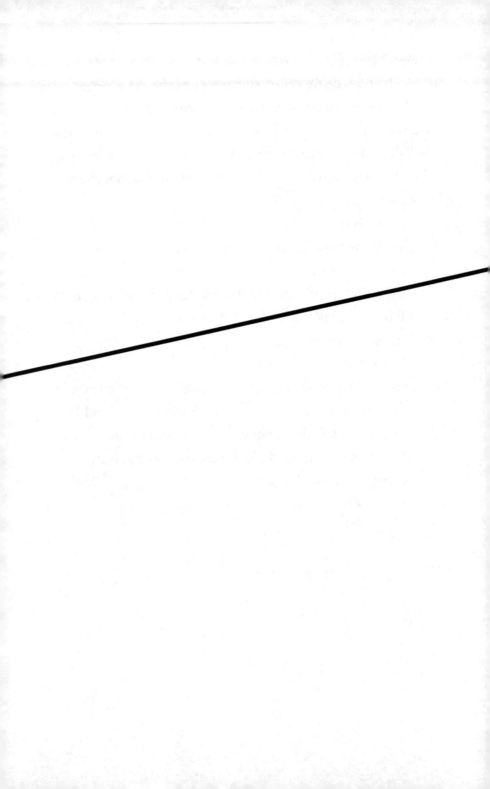

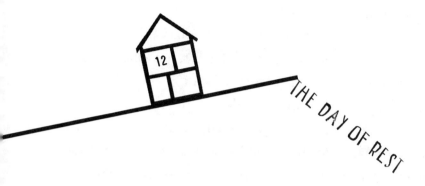

ON **S**ATURDAY, THE **D**AY OF **R**EST, **C**ALEB WAS IN A GOOD MOOD.

He drew up the blinds in the kitchen and let in the sunlight. He had Mom cut up a bowlful of apples, which the family ate with peanut butter. When she pointed out he'd gotten peanut butter in his beard, he chuckled.

Jory was in a good mood, too. The Mendoza twins hadn't been at school Thursday. Jory had spotted them in the schoolyard on Friday—but as soon as they'd seen him, they'd scurried away. Like they were suddenly afraid.

It made Jory wonder. Caleb hardly ever interfered with school stuff—home was home and school was school. And the twins *looked* fine. They certainly hadn't been buried up to their necks in a red ant pile in the hottest part of the desert, like Jory had fantasized more than a few times. But he decided not to ask Caleb if he'd gotten involved, in case he was wrong.

Or in case he was right.

Digging on Thursday and Friday had seemed easier, too. His shovel had felt lighter. The dirt, not quite so hard-packed. Jory suspected he was building up muscles. New ones, to go with the calluses under his gloves.

For lunch on Saturday, the family ate MREs. MRE stood for "Meal Ready-to-Eat," Caleb explained. The same thing he and his fellow soldiers ate when they were stationed abroad. It was fun peeling open the foil packages. Even if the food inside didn't taste all that good.

The family spent the afternoon sitting in the patio, drinking milk made from powder and playing games. Not Worldbuilding but Survival: Caleb's favorite. The family named survival scenarios—a hurricane, enemy aircraft, an influenza epidemic—and discussed what they'd do to stay alive.

Sometimes the game seemed sinister. Fateful, almost. Jory could practically see the superstorm lashing against the windows, hear the dark planes buzzing overhead, feel a cough tickling his throat.

Today, the game was funny.

They'd just finished orangutans escaped from the zoo and rain turned to Kool-Aid. Mom was laughing, and Caleb's eyes twinkled over his beard. "Zombie invasion," he said. "Go."

"First, you dig a hole in the ground . . ." Mom began.

The family laughed.

"Are they fast zombies, or the slow staggery kind?" Jory asked.

"Fifty-fifty," Caleb said.

"Then . . . you hide. Because eventually, they'll eat everybody. Everybody who's not hiding. And then they won't have anyone left to eat, and they'll starve."

"Very good." Caleb smiled. "We might survive the zombies yet."

Jory lurched toward Ansel with his arms out, growling. Ansel smiled. Then Jory turned and roared at Kit, who was wrapped in her flowered blanket. She rolled her eyes, then smiled, too. Maybe things were okay between them now.

He'd watched her closely since Wednesday night—ever since his dream. Her eyes were definitely eye-shaped. Larger than average, but ordinary. If it hadn't been a dream—and Jory felt pretty sure it *had* been—the star-eyes part must have been a hallucination, a trick of shadow and moonlight. Her voice, an illusion of wind.

"All right, Jory," Caleb said. "Your turn. What's the danger now?"

Jory thought. "How about aliens?"

The smile in his stepdad's eyes dimmed the slightest bit. "Okay," he agreed. "Aliens."

"What kind of aliens?" Mom asked. "Friendly ones, or . . . ?"

Caleb shook his head. "You'd never know. Not until they arrived. You probably couldn't imagine them—what they looked like. What they acted like. What they could do to you."

"But how would we know they were dangerous?" Jory asked.

"Why else would they arrive on our planet?"

"Maybe . . . to explore."

"Name one explorer who didn't have ill in his heart. Tearing apart the land. Searching for gold or silver. Enslaving the natives."

Charles Darwin, Jory thought. He explored the Galapagos Islands, discovering species. Or astronauts— their journeys into space were about discovery too, weren't they? Then again, he could think up plenty of ill-hearted *what ifs*.

What if Darwin did it all for fame and fortune?

What if astronauts stole moon rocks to sell on the black market?

What if . . .

"Of course, most aliens wouldn't be dangerous," Caleb went on. "Just like humans. Most people are just trying to get by—here on earth, anyway. But it's the ones in charge we'd have to fear. And it's the ones in charge who'd make it to our planet first."

"The Officials," Mom said.

Caleb nodded. "Whatever their version of Officials is."

Then he nodded at Kit. "Better hope those Officials don't come for you, too."

For a moment, the family was silent, unsure whether Caleb was joking. Then Mom forced a chuckle. "Don't worry, Kit," she said. "We'd never let that happen."

"Never!" Jory agreed.

Caleb just sat there, smiling with his eyes.

The sun still shone through the patio windows, but the room seemed darker. Jory felt responsible—he'd come up with the topic, hadn't he? He should have said killer unicorns or evil clowns or something totally preposterous. Then again, he'd thought aliens were preposterous, too.

Always watch the sky, Caleb had said.

Jory glanced at Kit. Her eyes were still eye-shaped, but her jaw was set. Her cheeks glowed pink. She met Jory's gaze for an instant. Then she reached for her glass of chocolate milk—and knocked it onto the ground.

Caleb stood so fast his chair tumbled over. "What's the matter with you?" he bellowed.

Ansel burst into tears. Caleb rarely ever yelled, and his thundering voice was a shock. "I'm sure it was an accident—" Mom began, looking distressed.

"It wasn't an accident. I saw the entire thing. That girl did it on purpose."

Jory jumped up and grabbed the roll of paper towels. His hands shook as he sopped up Kit's milk.

"Go to your room," Caleb ordered Kit.

Slowly, she stood, still wrapped in the cocoon of her flowered blanket.

"Wait," Caleb said. "You should give Ansel that blanket. He's shivering."

Despite his tears, Ansel looked cozy enough on Mom's lap. But Jory knew better than to argue. Kit hesitated, her brow creased and her lower lip sticking out. *Give it to him,* Jory thought. Finally, she unwound her blanket from her shoulders and handed it to Caleb. Jory exhaled.

Caleb draped the blanket over Ansel. "Thank you," he said. "Now go."

———

The rest of the weekend passed slowly, with the family's good mood gone.

Jory tried to play Worldbuilding with Kit. Instead of painting her handmade house with her usual flamboyance, she painted it dark purple. All four walls and the roof, too.

"Well, that's depressing," Jory said.

She stuck out her tongue at him, then turned and flounced away.

Jory rinsed their paintbrushes. He felt sorry for Kit—but also kind of annoyed. Because it *really had* seemed like she'd knocked over her milk on purpose. And if that was true . . . well, what had she expected?

He cleaned the kitchen with Mom, who seemed subdued.

Jory wondered if the volume of Caleb's voice still echoed in her ears, too.

He even took Ansel for a walk in the fields. Or tried to. They only made it twenty feet before Ansel sat down in the dirt and refused to go farther.

Jory sat beside him. "The sky's so blue today," he tried. "No clouds for Cloudwatching. But you don't know what that is. Hey, look!" Jory pointed out a hawk circling overhead. "That's a hawk. Watch out, it might snatch you up."

Ansel scowled.

"Kit would have thought that was funny," Jory said. That was the problem, he thought. He had no idea how to make Ansel laugh. Was Caleb the missing link? Ansel was Caleb's real child. Jory and Kit weren't. On some level, that had to count.

Jory snatched a rock from Ansel's hands before he could put it in his mouth. His wail made Jory grimace. Whenever Ansel cried, his face turned a shocking shade of plum.

"Better stop," Jory warned, "or I'll sell you to the Officials."

He felt bad immediately, but Ansel didn't seem to understand. Finally, Jory lugged him back to the house.

Sunday afternoon, Jory attempted to work on his tunnels project, but he couldn't concentrate. He still wasn't sure what to write about—there were too many possibilities. Tunnels were so much more than elongated holes in the ground. They had a purpose. They led to something.

But what was the something?

His topic was too broad, he decided. He needed more Internet time to whittle it into shape, but the computer line at school was always endless.

It would make *much* more sense to use Alice's computer again.

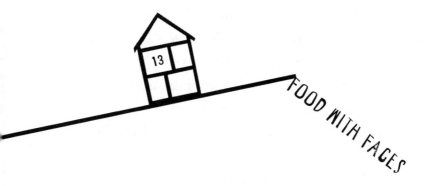

13

FOOD WITH FACES

By the time Jory felt brave enough to knock on Alice's door, it was nearly dinnertime.

"Well, look what we have here!" she exclaimed. She had on the same dress and sneakers she'd worn to school that day, except she'd traded her big plaid coat for a purple bathrobe.

Jory shuffled his feet. "Um, hi."

"So, Jory Birch. What's your story?"

"Huh?"

"Why are you standing on my doorstep, looking all sheepish?"

Jory wondered if sheepish was better than owlish. "Well, I was hoping for some computer time. And . . . are you guys having dinner tonight?"

"We plan on eating, yeah."

"Right. I meant, um . . ."

"Relax, I know what you meant. We're about to eat right now, actually." Alice grinned, then hollered, "DAD! Is there enough food for my friend Jory Birch to eat with us?"

It hadn't occurred to Jory that there might not be enough food. He should have asked yesterday—or earlier today, at school. He should have come an hour ago. "I can just use the computer, if there isn't—"

"OF COURSE!" Mr. Diaz yelled back.

"Are you sure?" Jory asked. "Is he sure? Because . . ."

"Jory! It's getting old." She grabbed his arm. "Unfortunately, all we're having is leftover vegetarian lasagna. Which means there isn't even *meat* in it . . ."

In the kitchen, Mr. Diaz was slicing lasagna with a pizza cutter. He set it down to shake Jory's hand. "A pleasure to meet you, Mr. Birch," he said formally. "I apologize in advance for the wilted lasagna. Our oven is ancient and temperamental."

"Lucky for you, you'll get a brand-new one soon," Alice said.

"At your new house?" Jory asked.

Mr. Diaz nodded. "If the development ever finishes! Anyway, this lasagna's not just wilted, but vegetarian. My wife is on another meat cleanse."

"What's a . . . meat cleanse?"

"It's when my mom gets all sentimental about food with faces," Alice explained. "After just three days, she'll crave a burger, and—"

"I heard that!" Mrs. Brooks entered the room. She honked one of Alice's hair buns like a clown horn. "I'll have you know, it's not about faces. Sometimes one burger can be made with the meat of a thousand cows, all ground up together, did you know that?"

It sounded like something Caleb might say. Jory wondered if Mrs. Brooks also listened to any of Caleb's talk-radio programs.

"I could eat a thousand cows right now," Mr. Diaz said.

Mrs. Brooks handed him a stack of plates. "Then let's get this show on the road, lasagna man."

Alice had to push Jory into the dining room and point at a chair. He felt like all three of them were staring at him, even when they weren't.

"So, Alice tells us you live on a farm?" Mr. Diaz asked.

Jory tried not to groan. "Well, not like a *farm* farm. It used to be one, but we don't have animals or anything."

"Ah," Mr. Diaz said.

Jory smiled tightly, bracing for more follow-up questions. But Mr. Diaz directed his next question to the entire table.

"If you could have any type of farm in the world," he asked, "what would you have?"

"Miniature horses," Alice declared. "No question. Also Shetland ponies. And Shetland sheepdogs."

"I always thought it'd be nice to grow flowers," Mr. Diaz said.

Alice raised her eyebrows. "Isn't that just a garden?"

"Where do you think all those bouquets in the supermarket come from? No, I'd grow entire fields of flowers. Poppies, lilies, wildflowers."

"Once you farm a wildflower," Mrs. Brooks said, "it's not wild anymore, is it?"

"Oh yeah? Then what would you farm?"

"Ostriches. You can ride them! I saw it on the Discovery Channel."

"That doesn't seem very comfortable," Mr. Diaz said.

"Why not?" Mrs. Brooks said. "Your seat would be padded with feathers."

"What exactly would you be *farming*, though?" Alice asked. "Don't farms need a purpose? Would you eat the ostriches?"

"Of course not!"

"Ostriches have faces," Mr. Diaz said knowingly. "Off-limits for consumption."

Alice grabbed a bottle of hot sauce, leaned over the table, and squirted a smiley face on her mom's lasagna. "What're you gonna do now?"

Everybody at the table laughed, Jory included. Their

conversation was so playful, so joyful. No tension. No talk about digging or danger.

Jory wondered what his family was doing right this minute.

Sleeping, probably.

He wondered if that was why he didn't miss them.

———

After dinner, Jory sat beside Alice on the front porch as she restrung the laces on her sneakers. "I can never get these dumb things right," she complained. "They're either too tight, or too loose."

"Maybe you should get some boots," Jory suggested. "Mine have zippers up the sides. See? I can put them on really quickly, if I need to."

Alice yanked on her laces, then turned to him. "Can I ask you a question?"

"I don't know. Maybe."

"Don't get offended. But—is there a reason you dress that way?"

"Look who's talking. Isn't that a bathrobe?"

Alice sniffed. "Anything goes for around-the-house apparel. I'm talking about your big ol' monster boots. And those crazy pants. All the buckles and pockets and snaps. Alfonso Mendoza says—and I know he's human waste, it's not like I *believe* him, okay—but he says maybe they're for, like, weapons." She squinted at him. "Don't get offended. Are you offended?"

"They're not for weapons!"

"I know. That's what I told him." Alice paused. "But then what are they for?"

"They're for . . ."

Well, the boots were for tramping around in the canyon, obviously. But Jory couldn't say that. And he didn't know the exact purpose of the buckles and pockets and snaps. They were another thing Caleb had never explained—but he could guess.

"They're for being prepared," he said finally.

"Prepared for what?"

Jory wished someone had taught Alice to keep her questions inside her head. Or that he had a simple answer to give her. "You know my stepfather, Caleb?"

"I don't *know* him, but yeah, you mentioned him."

"He thinks . . ." Jory swallowed. "He thinks something is coming."

Instantly, he felt guilty. Like Caleb was standing behind him, peering over his shoulder. But he felt relieved, too. Like a tiny pin had breached the balloon in his chest. It didn't burst—but almost imperceptibly, the pressure let up.

"What kind of something?" Alice asked.

"Something dangerous."

"What kind of something dangerous?"

He shook his head. "Caleb doesn't share many details. At least not with me and my sister."

"I didn't know you had a sister!"

Jory tried to keep a straight face. He couldn't believe he'd mentioned Kit! He'd gotten too comfortable after their dinnertime conversation, his stomach full of Mr. Diaz's lasagna. He took a deep breath, trying to act like it wasn't a big deal. "She's younger," he said. "And homeschooled."

"Oh. Is she—"

"Anyway," he interrupted, "Caleb knows things, but he's careful about what he tells us. Sometimes I think it's war— he was a soldier, so he's able to predict that kind of thing. If not war, or *normal* war, maybe it's something like . . ." He lowered his voice. "Aliens."

Alice's eyes grew large enough to rival Kit's. "Aliens?"

"I don't know. There are signs."

"Like the green kind of aliens? Or the gray kind? Or giant robots or lizards or insect monsters or what?"

"Come on! That's ridiculous."

"You're the one who brought aliens into this!"

"Not me—Caleb. And it's not like he said, 'The aliens are coming!' It's just something I've wondered about, because he always tells us to watch the sky, and that's why . . ." Now Jory started to feel ridiculous. "It's probably not aliens. I'm sure it's not."

"Your stepfather sounds kind of crazy," Alice said. "I'm sorry! Don't look at me like that. But he does."

"You don't know anything."

She shrugged. "Maybe I don't."

"There are *signs*," Jory insisted. "Caleb's really smart. Like off-the-charts-IQ kind of smart, Mom says. One of the best soldiers there ever was, even if his superior officers didn't always know it. He's done the research. He knows what he's talking about. And even if—even if the something bad *didn't* come, what's the problem with being prepared?"

He sat back, feeling smug.

"I guess there's no problem," Alice replied. "But then again—how much time do you spend preparing for the . . . something? For the future?"

"I don't know. A fair amount."

She shoved back her bathrobe cuffs thoughtfully. "I used to be really big on environmental stuff. Remember last year in fifth grade? When Mrs. Feinberg made me the Earth Crusader? I used to lie awake at night thinking of ice caps and polar bears, and the chopped-down rain forests, and that huge dead spot in the Gulf of Mexico because of farm poisons seeping into the sea. I'd think about how the world was for sure going to freeze or catch on fire or whatever. I'd even, like, cry about it." She smiled self-consciously. "Sometimes I still want to.

"Nowadays, I recycle and take short showers and stuff. Plus I fully intend to become an ecological cryptozoologist someday."

"An eco-*what*? Is that an actual thing?"

Alice ignored him. "But I realized something. When you spend so much of your life worried about the future . . . you forget to *live*."

Jory wanted to shake his head. He was living right this minute, wasn't he? His heart was beating and everything. But he was pretty sure that wasn't what Alice was talking about.

"I just don't see the point of being so scared all the time," she said. "You know?"

He had to laugh. "Oh yeah? What about all that talk of bones and ghosts and chalk-white faces, huh?"

"That's just fun."

Fun. It wasn't a word Caleb used very often. Or any of the family. It felt like ages since he'd spent real time with Kit, the way they used to. There was no time for fun anymore, other than Survival, and that hadn't ended well. Jory's head began to hurt. Not that he'd *never* questioned Caleb before. But it made him feel nervous, every time. As if Caleb wasn't just standing behind Jory, peering over his shoulder—but a *part* of him, inhabiting his skin.

"It's getting late," Jory said quietly. "Thanks for dinner. Thank your parents again for me, okay?"

"Don't you need to use the computer?"

"Maybe another time." He stuffed his hands in his pockets and took a few steps down the sidewalk. Then he turned and came back.

"Hey, Alice . . ."

"Yeah?"

"A minute ago, you said something about forgetting to *live*."

She nodded.

"What exactly did you mean?"

Alice's grin grew until it stretched across her whole face. "Do you really want to know?"

14

ALIVE

"TRASH?" JORY WRINKLED HIS NOSE.

They stood behind the hardware store in the waning light. Alice was balanced on a wooden pallet, rifling through a trash bin overstuffed with boxes. "Cardboard," she corrected him.

"So, trash."

Alice threw him a haughty look. "One person's trash is another person's treasure, Jory Birch. Haven't you ever made a cardboard box into a spaceship? Don't you have any imagination?"

"Of course I have one." He paused. "My sister and I make things out of wood scraps sometimes."

"Things like what?"

"Houses. Towns."

Jory nudged a piece of gravel with his toe. He felt like

he'd betrayed his family's trust again, even though they were only talking about games. *Kit wouldn't mind*, he told himself. In fact, she'd probably *love* Alice Brooks-Diaz—her outrageous ideas, her bizarre fascinations.

Jory cleared his throat. "Need any help?" he asked Alice.

She was leaning so far over the trash can, Jory worried she'd fall inside. "Oh, this one's perfect!" she exclaimed, righting herself and hopping off the pallet. She shoved a rectangle of cardboard at Jory.

It said TANGER.

Jory looked at Alice quizzically.

"Probably belonged to some tangerines," she explained. "It's not important. The shape's what's important, and the stiffness. Too stiff, and it won't slide right. Too floppy, and you'll possibly shatter your tailbone. Which would make sitting in class really problematic, don't you think?"

"Hey!"

Erik Dixon strolled toward them, grinning. His bouncy gait made Jory think of walking on the moon. Jory raised his hand to wave, then scratched his head instead.

"What are you guys doing?" Erik said.

"I'm taking him sledding." Alice brandished a wedge of cardboard.

Sledding? She had to be joking again—it got cold where they lived, but rarely snowed. Erik knew exactly what she meant, though. "The slopes!" he exclaimed. "For real? Have you done it before?"

"Thousands of times," Alice boasted. "Jory here is a newbie, though."

Jory resented being called a newbie, but he kept quiet.

"Man oh man," Erik said. "You're gonna love it."

Instead of leaving, he stood there, watching. Jory didn't get it. It wasn't like Erik had nothing better to do. He probably had nine guys sitting on his front porch right now, waiting to play baseball or badminton or whatever it was they did after school.

Alice glanced at Jory, eyebrows raised. He shrugged.

"Erik Dixon," she said, "would you like to hit the slopes with us?"

Erik grinned even wider. "I thought you'd never ask."

———

It's not like they were *that* high.

They'd walked six blocks and climbed two rickety staircases shaded by eucalyptus trees—a different grove than the one Jory walked through daily. These trees felt taller, because of the way they staggered up the hillside. More like an actual forest.

Once they reached the top of the hill, Erik nudged Jory with his elbow. "This view over that way is my all-time favorite."

Jory turned to look. "*Wow,*" he said. He wove through

the trees until they ended, and there was nothing around him but air.

It's not like they were *that* high. But he felt on top of the world.

Jory grinned as the wind picked up, whooshing against his face. No, it wasn't the wind. It was the sky itself. Ruffling his hair with sunset-colored fingers. He stretched his arms, and they seemed to go up and up and up.

No ceiling.

No dirt.

Nothing but air and sky and whatever came after that, stretching on and on into infinity. It made his town seem tiny, even though he could see more of it than he ever had.

He stepped closer to the edge. He could see their school. The factory where Caleb worked. The new housing development at the edge of town, where Alice was planning to move. Its partially finished homes looked like Kit and his Worldbuilding game come to life. He could also see lots of canyons from the hilltop: gouged into the landscape in curves and zigzags. Some looked broad, others deep. Still others were so choked with brush he couldn't guess their size.

"I think that's my house," he said suddenly.

Erik stood next to him. "The little rusty-looking one?"

Jory laughed. "No, the big brown one beside it. The reddish one's our barn."

"So you really *do* live on a farm?"

"Technically it's a farm. I mean, it might have been some-body else's farm, before my stepdad bought the house. But we don't have any animals. And the crops are just for us."

"Crops?" Alice asked.

"Cucumbers. Squash. Mom preserves them, so we have . . . Whatever, it's boring." Jory grabbed a piece of cardboard. "Are we going to do this thing, or what?"

Erik grinned and grabbed a second piece. "If you like the taste of dust. Because you two are going to *eat* mine."

Jory started to follow Erik, then hesitated. "Alice?"

She was still looking at Jory's house. "Don't get all antsy pantsy," she said. "I'm coming."

The slopes turned out to be a trio of cement slides, angling steeply down the hillside. They'd been there for decades, Alice explained. Ever since her parents were kids. Jory saw no rails, or anything to hold on to. His stomach flip-flopped.

Erik and Alice didn't seem nervous, though. They were already kicking off their shoes. Jory started to unzip his boots. He paused, feeling even more apprehensive. Then he rezipped them.

"Stinky feet," Erik said knowingly.

From the bottom, the slides hadn't looked that steep. Another illusion. As he settled on top of TANGER, Jory dis-covered the descent had quintupled.

"I'm going to break every bone in my body," he said, "aren't I."

"Probably," Erik said.

"Most likely, yes," Alice agreed.

"Thought so." Jory shook his head. What was he doing here? He was seeking out danger when the rest of his life was about avoiding it, preparing for it. Anything to stay safe. Now Jory felt pulled by twin magnets. One tugging him home, where his family slept. One holding him right here—in the real world, with kids who might possibly become his *friends*.

"Are you ready?" Alice asked.

Jory held his eyes closed a moment, then opened them. "If this is what *living* means, I guess . . ."

He pushed off.

—

It was the longest five seconds of his life.

When his brain vibrated back into place, Jory rolled over and sat up. There was mud in his eye. His mouth tasted like eucalyptus. "That was . . ." He spit out a leaf. "Wow. That was wild. That was so crazy, I don't even . . . wow. Just wow. *What?*"

Erik and Alice were cracking up.

"Come on, guys. Are there leaves in my hair?"

They only laughed harder. "No, you're just—your reaction," Alice said finally. "We're laughing because you're, like, a bubble of glee."

"I was laughing at the leaves in his hair," Erik said.

Jory followed them back up the hill to collect their shoes. The climb seemed shorter this time—maybe because he was practically skipping.

"Want to go again?" Alice asked at the top.

Go again? Seriously? It was stupid and it was dangerous and he could have broken every bone in his body. And it was the most alive he'd ever felt. "Yeah! But—one sec."

Jory began to unzip his boots.

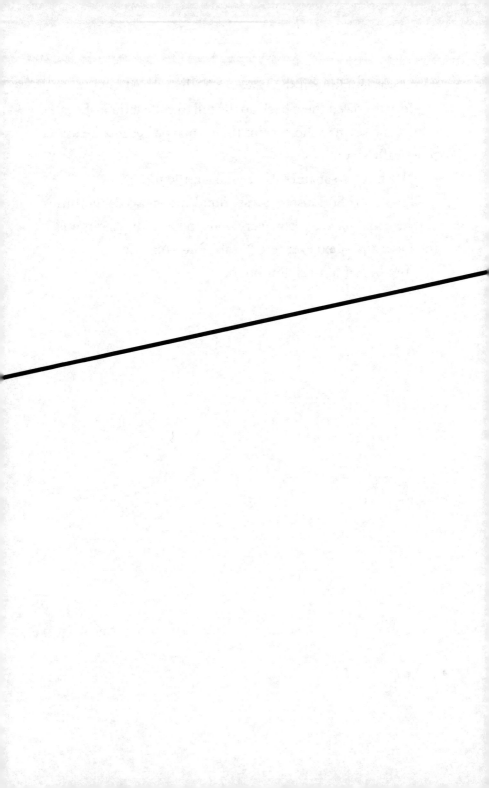

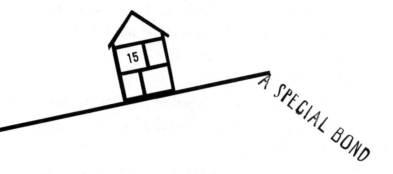

15

A SPECIAL BOND

THE SLOPES CHANGED EVERYTHING.

Well, maybe not *everything*. But for the first time, Jory found himself looking forward to school—not just the classroom parts, but also the parts before and after and in between. The parts he usually dreaded.

Like lunchtime. Alice sat across from Jory halfway through lunch, as usual, but now Erik stopped by to chat. One time Sam Kapur and Randall Loomis joined in, too. They weren't that bad, when Randall wasn't talking about making out with supermodels.

On Wednesday, Jory walked home with Alice.

On Thursday, he stood on Erik's porch and talked about comic books for not quite twenty minutes, but definitely more than fifteen. Erik couldn't believe Jory hadn't read any. "Not even *X-Men*?" he asked. "What about, like, *Superman*—everybody's read some of those. No? Seriously?"

On Friday, Jory chatted with both of them so long he had to run the rest of the way home. The black-and-white dog barked as he sprinted over the bridge.

"Sorry!" he shouted. "No time!"

Every evening, when Jory kicked off his combat boots and crawled into bed, he was certain he'd fall asleep instantly. One, two, three, lights-out.

But every evening, he lay awake, eyes scanning the dark ceiling. Body exhausted, but brain turned on—thinking of Alice, and Erik, and the slopes, and everything they'd talked about. There was always something new to go over. Something to fill the too-short hours before Mom woke him to dig again.

"You seem distracted," Mom said in the canyon that night. "Is everything okay?"

Jory realized he'd been leaning on his shovel, lost in thought. "Everything's fine," he replied. "I'm just a little tired." Not the whole truth, but not a lie.

"Me too. Good thing tomorrow's our Day of Rest, right?" She smiled, wiping her brow with her forearm. Then she headed toward the tunnel, one hand on the small of her back.

Jory watched her go, recalling the painful backaches she had suffered at the coffee shop. Then, she hadn't been digging—she'd only been carrying trays filled with coffees.

The occasional sandwich. He used to feel so protective of her. Now, he didn't need to—Caleb had taken over that role.

Which was *good*, of course. The best thing that had ever happened to them.

But sometimes—if Jory was entirely honest with himself—he found himself missing those early days. Not the tiny apartment, filled with the ache of Dad's absence. Or the crummy coffee shop, with Mom's shiny-bald boss. But he missed their closeness, when the family was just him and Mom. The two of them versus the world.

As he snipped roots with a pair of shears, he wondered what would happen if he told her about Alice and Erik. About the slopes. About Alice's parents and the way they joked at dinner.

The idea made him feel uneasy.

He wasn't doing anything wrong, he reasoned. Tuesdays were his off days. What did it matter if he was reenergizing at home, or at Alice's house? What did it matter who he talked to at school, or after? He still came home every day. He still dug nightly. He even did his homework in the gap between school and dinner . . . when he used to play with Kit.

He glanced over at her now: a skinny, dark-haired shadow in too-large gloves, yanking at weeds. He'd play with her again, he promised himself. As soon as he caught up.

When he wasn't so *tired*.

—

"I have to go to the supermarket," Mom announced on Saturday.

She said it boldly, standing with her arms crossed in the kitchen. But Jory knew better.

Mom hated the supermarket. She'd complained about it dozens of times. The fluorescent lights, and the way they bounced blindingly off the floors. The people who jostled past her with their overstuffed carts. And the *food*—so many different kinds of food, with confusing labels wrapped around every box and can. Food in towers that looked like they might topple over, which made Jory picture Mom buried in an aluminum pile of green beans and creamed corn.

Caleb went, most of the time. Or Jory would grab a couple of items from the convenience store on his way home from school. The family didn't need much—the fields provided almost everything.

"I thought Saturday was our Day of Rest?" Jory said.

"Your stepdad's working," Mom said. "And I'm all out of salt. These winter squash will go bad if I don't preserve them this afternoon. Do you mind watching Ansel?"

Jory glanced at his little brother, who sat in a high chair, swinging his legs. He had a smear of peanut butter on his cheek. "Okay, but . . . are you sure you don't want me to go?"

Mom nodded. "I have other errands to run. Anyway, you should spend more time playing together. Brothers have a special bond, after all."

Jory wasn't too sure about that. "I guess," he said,

following her to the door. "But . . . how will you carry every-thing?"

"Caleb will pick me up on his way home from the fac-tory."

"Then why don't you wait for him and go together?"

Mom stopped and looked at Jory. "You don't think I can handle this myself?"

"That's not what I meant, I—"

"It's okay, Jory. I like that you worry about me." She smiled. "I'll be fine."

Once she was gone, Jory approached his little brother. Ansel stopped swinging his legs and stared at Jory warily.

"So," Jory said. "What do you want to do? Any games you want to play?"

Ansel's forehead crinkled. "No," he said, in his chipmunk-on-helium voice.

"Want to go outside? It's nice and warm out, and—"

"No."

"Are you sure?"

"No."

Jory paused. "Does that mean you're sure, or you're not sure?"

Ansel scrunched up his whole face. "No!"

Jory sighed, exasperated. "Fine! We'll go play in the canyon, how would you like that? We'll dig all day and all night and all day again—"

Ansel began to cry.

"Shhh," Jory said. He didn't want Mom and Caleb to come home to a plum-faced toddler. "I was just kidding! We'll stay right here. We can do whatever you want . . ."

But Ansel wouldn't stop bawling. Jory began opening cupboards frantically, hoping to uncover a magic solution. Like a stash of multicolored cupcakes. Or a glittery fairy godmother with a scream-stopping wand. Nothing but food in jars, cans, and pouches.

When he closed the refrigerator, he saw Kit standing in the doorway.

He felt a flash of guilt. By now, over a week had passed since they'd spent any real time together. "Mom's at the supermarket," he explained. "I can't get him to stop crying."

Kit twisted her mouth, like she was trying not to laugh.

"I'm glad you find this amusing," Jory said gruffly. He unscrewed a jar of pickles and offered one to Ansel. Ansel only grew more upset, which wasn't surprising because, well, pickles. Jory closed the jar and plugged his ears. His brother's face verged on red by now, with plum on the horizon.

"Maybe we can give him one of our Worldbuilding houses to play with?" Jory suggested. "We could . . ."

He trailed off when he saw Kit's expression.

"Sorry, I know that's our game. But he just—" He motioned to Ansel, as if his wails weren't filling the room. "Have any ideas?"

Kit raised her eyebrows, as if asking *Who, me?*

Jory knew it was a last resort. If he and Ansel didn't have

much of a relationship, Kit and Ansel's was almost non-existent. Probably because Caleb never let her watch him. At this rate, though, Mom and Caleb wouldn't want Jory to watch him either. And then Mom wouldn't be able to run any other errands Caleb needed her to, and . . . Jory didn't want to think beyond that.

"Anything," he begged. "Anything at all."

Kit nodded, looking resolute. Then she crossed the kitchen and stopped in front of Ansel. She leaned in, so her face was just a few inches from Ansel's screaming one. He continued to wail, but his eyes were curious, almost rapt.

Jory watched with his mouth half open. What was going on? Should he stop her? He knew Kit would never hurt Ansel—but she looked so *intense*. Maybe there was a reason Caleb never asked her to babysit. "Kit . . ." he began.

Kit ignored him. Slowly, she reached out and mussed up Ansel's wispy, pale hair.

When she drew her hands away, it stood on end.

Jory stared in amazement. He blinked, then rubbed his eyes. When he opened them, his brother's hair was still sticking out in every direction, as if electrified. Ansel must have felt a tickle, because he swiped at his head, touching his hair. It surprised him so much he stopped crying altogether. Then he began to giggle. It was so weird, and wild, and impossible, but Jory couldn't help himself. He burst out laughing.

And then Kit laughed too.

She clapped a hand over her mouth, as if startled by her own voice. Ansel and Jory froze mid-guffaw, staring at her. The room was silent.

Then all three of them started to laugh again—hilariously, hysterically. They collapsed on their backs and rolled on the floor and wiped tears from their eyes. And they laughed, and laughed, and laughed.

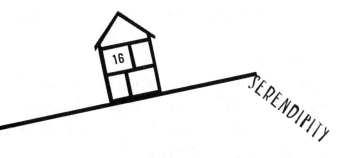

16

SERENDIPITY

Jory thought he'd catch up on sleep that night. Back to his regularly scheduled slumber. But again, he found himself staring at the ceiling. This time, he wasn't thinking about Alice or Erik and their conversations.

He was thinking about Kit.

He couldn't get the sound of her laughter out of his head. Bright and shrill and a little hoarse, though not as hoarse as he'd have expected. Had she been holding it in this whole time, just waiting for the humor? Had nothing been worth laughing at, until now?

Finally, Jory climbed out of bed. He tiptoed downstairs in his stocking feet, carrying his boots under his arm. He didn't want to wake Caleb. Or Mom, who'd brought home another migraine along with the pickling salt. He shut the back door quietly behind him.

The night, once alien, felt familiar now. The prickly chill in the air. The crickets screeching in the fields. The starlight lacing the edges of the clouds. Familiar—but not comforting.

And never safe.

As he zipped his boots, Jory wondered if a person could ever get used to darkness. If a person could ever stop squinting into the shadows. Double-taking at every tremble of weeds. Freezing at every cracked stick and giggle.

Jory froze.

Every *giggle*?

The sound came again. So soft he could barely hear it over the cricketsong. He scanned the fields, wondering if he'd misheard—the mewl of a lost kitten, maybe, or a quiet whine from the black-and-white dog.

Then he saw Kit.

She sat with her back against the barn, her flowered blanket draped over her shoulders. Jory was glad to see she'd retrieved it from Ansel. She wore her ballet slippers—a real mess, now—and cradled one of their Worldbuilding houses on her lap. He felt nervous as he approached. Which was silly, because this was Kit. His little sister. The person he knew best—who knew *him* best.

"So that was you giggling?" he asked, standing over her.

Kit shrugged one shoulder. She stayed silent, but the giggle lingered in her eyes.

"What's so funny?"

She poked one hand out from under the flowered blanket and pointed at Jory.

"Oh, thanks a lot." He grinned, feeling a sudden lightness. He hadn't realized how much he'd missed her over the last few busy days. "I love how you're acting like this is no big deal. After I haven't heard your voice in what, nearly three years?" Then Jory froze again. "Wait a second—if you can laugh, doesn't it mean you can speak, too?"

He knew it was true. Kit's vocal cords worked. She could listen and read. She knew the words. She just had to *say* them.

"Will you try?" he asked. "For me?"

Kit peered up at him, her head tilted, her blackbird hair falling over one shoulder. Then she nodded. She nodded again, even more determinedly. She took a deep breath. She opened her mouth.

"Hold on!" Jory exclaimed.

He knelt in front of her. "If this is truly the first time you're going to speak in almost three whole years, your first word needs to be memorable. It needs to be epic."

She looked at him like he was crazy.

"How about a really fun word, like . . ." Jory thought. "Like 'salamander.' Or 'onomatopoeia'—that's when a word sounds like what it describes. *Bark* or *oink*, for example." He laughed. "Maybe *oink* should be your first word?"

She bonked him in the shoulder with her Worldbuilding house.

"Or how about serendipity?" he suggested. "That's a good one. That's one of my favorites. It's when something wonderful happens when you don't expect it. A happy surprise. Like you! The day you showed up in the pumpkin field was a happy surprise. It was serendipity."

Kit rolled her eyes. "*Jory!*" she said.

She *said*.

And she'd said *his name*.

"Great choice!" Jory exclaimed, beaming so hard his cheeks ached. "Best word ever. And you can't take it back. You've said it—it's written in the stars."

Kit's laughter sounded like music.

"And now I know what your voice sounds like! I was starting to think it sounded like *this*," he said, making his voice as deep as he could. "Or like *this*." Now he spoke in a falsetto.

"You're ridiculous," Kit said.

How astonishing it was: her voice. Raspy from disuse, but all hers.

Jory didn't want to do anything that could possibly quell that marvelous sound. He knew he should take it easy. He knew he should remain calm. But his heart was soaring! He couldn't help it. He grabbed Kit's hand and pulled her up.

And together, they danced. Skipping, stumbling, jumping, leaping, hand in hand, just the way they always had— except this time, both of them laughed out loud. Above them, the stars seemed to dance, too, glittering ellipses that swirled in the sky. A second meteor shower of their very own.

All too soon, Jory felt dizzy and had to stop. Still laughing, he crawled toward the barn and leaned against it. Kit kept dancing, her skinny arms sweeping the sky. She leaped and twirled, those impossibly perfect spins she must have mastered *somewhere*.

Jory realized, for the first time, he could ask.

"Hey, Kit," he said, and she skidded to a stop. "Where'd you learn to dance like that?"

She shrugged.

"Maybe you'll tell me later. Right? Now that you're talking to me? Why'd you decide to wait this long to speak, anyway?"

She shrugged again. His stubborn sister.

"I'm sure you had your reasons."

Kit joined him at the barn, sitting cross-legged atop her flowered blanket. She picked up her Worldbuilding house and replaced it in her lap.

Jory cleared his throat. He brimmed with questions, but didn't want to overwhelm her. Especially if Kit couldn't put to words *why*. Why she'd stayed quiet all these months and years, ever since the serendipitous day he'd found her in the pumpkin field. The moment she'd spoken her last word: her name. That's the moment their story began. But what about Kit's own story?

What about *before*?

It wasn't that Jory had never wondered about it. But he

had thought he'd never get an answer. Thinking about Kit's life before the pumpkin field made him feel anxious, unsettled. He wanted to reach backward into all those question marks and bring her home.

"Kit . . ." he began slowly. "How much do you remember from before? Before you got here?"

Her silence went on so long, Jory glanced at her. She was turning the wooden house in her hands. It was the one with the purple walls, he noticed.

"I don't know," she said finally.

"Anything at all? You were little, but—maybe some image, some kind of memory—"

"It was hot," Kit said. "There were other kids there."

"Other kids? What do you mean? Like an orphanage, or . . . ?"

"I don't know," Kit said. "I don't remember."

Jory began to feel uneasy. "But you—"

"I don't want to talk about it anymore."

"All right." He nodded.

Even though Kit *had* to remember more than that. Right? She hadn't just tumbled from the sky. Burst into being like one of her shooting stars. He remembered how the meteors had vanished as suddenly as they'd sparked, and he had to swallow before he spoke again.

"You're awfully brave, coming out here at night," he said, thinking of the thunk he'd heard. "Sometimes I wonder if this barn's haunted."

"It's not haunted."

Kit said it so matter-of-factly, it made him wonder. "Why are you so sure?"

"Caleb works in it sometimes."

"Really?" It was strange, although Jory couldn't pinpoint exactly why. Caleb probably had tools in there, among the old poison junk. "Well, that doesn't mean it's not haunted."

Kit rolled her eyes. "Don't be so stubborn."

It made Jory smile, because he'd been thinking the same thing about her. Like sister, like brother. Another kind of special bond. In the time they'd spent together, at least.

Which wasn't very much time lately. A jolt of guilt stabbed through Jory's middle. "Listen, " he said. "I'm sorry I've been so busy lately. I'll do a better job hanging out with you, promise."

"Okay."

"Especially now that you're *talking* to me! Think of how much more fun Cloudwatching will be, now that I don't have to guess the creatures you point out."

"You're usually wrong," she said, yawning and stretching.

"Sleepy?"

She shrugged.

"We should probably get some rest. Tomorrow's a dig day, after all."

She exhaled noisily. "Digging's so boring," she said. "I'm sick of it. I *hate* it."

"Me too," Jory said.

Which wasn't a betrayal, he thought. It *wasn't*. Of course they hated digging—anybody in their right mind would hate it. Digging was the worst. Especially when they didn't know what it was for.

Would they ever find out?

Jory shook the thought out of his head. Now, *that* was a betrayal.

"I won't tell, you know," he said, helping her to her feet. "About any of this."

Kit nodded, like she didn't expect any less from him. She pulled the flowered blanket back over her shoulders, the purple and red Worldbuilding house nestled inside.

"Hey Kit," he said. "Before we go—why do *you* think we're digging?"

She shrugged. But Jory couldn't help noticing that just for an instant, her eyes flickered upward.

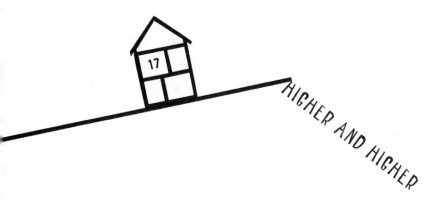

17

HIGHER AND HIGHER

JORY WAITED EAGERLY FOR KIT TO SPEAK AGAIN. As they headed downstairs together at midnight, clad in combats and cargoes. At breakfast on Monday. When they bumped into each other in the tunnel Monday night—Jory heading out, Kit heading in.

But she didn't say a word.

Jory figured it was because Mom and Caleb were never out of earshot. From time to time, Kit gave him a meaningful look. But then, her looks were always meaningful. For almost three years, they'd been her only language. Eyes widened and narrowed. Head tilts and shrugs. A sassy, stuck-out tongue, even after Jory joked that someday he'd pinch it off.

But now, Jory realized they were just . . . captions. Subtitles. Guesses, really. They only represented the surface of Kit's feelings. Even less of her thoughts.

And nothing of her memories.

Even if she didn't remember the details, she'd lived a whole six years before Jory and the family. A whole different life. Yet she spent all day, every day, in the farmhouse, the fields, and the canyon. No wonder she seemed upset that Jory had nights off weekly. That he had a life outside the family.

Maybe Kit wanted one, too.

—

On Tuesday, Jory jogged home from school. The long way, so Alice and Erik couldn't distract him. He'd already told Alice about his plan.

Caleb's truck was missing—good. Inside the farmhouse, the only sound was the lazy hum of the refrigerator. Mom and Ansel were fast asleep. Jory crept upstairs and knocked on Kit's door. When he opened it, he found her sitting up in bed, as if waiting for him to arrive. Her usual way of knowing things.

"Get dressed," he whispered. "I want you to come with me."

She stared at him.

"With me—and only me. Not Mom and Caleb. It's nothing scary. Nothing we're not allowed to do. I'm pretty sure, anyway." He was trying to convince himself along with Kit. "You can even wear your ballet slippers, if you want."

A slow smile spread across her face. "Really?" she whispered.

The sound of Kit's voice made Jory grin. Until that moment, a part of him thought he'd invented their talk Saturday night—that he'd dreamed it, like the stars in her eyes. "Really," he said. Kit dropped her flowered blanket on the bed and shoved her feet into her slippers.

Suddenly inspired, Jory rolled up Kit's blanket and stuck it under her sheet. He patted and prodded until it was sufficiently girl-shaped to fool Mom if she checked.

Together, they tiptoed into the narrow hallway. The stairs creaked as they crept down. Of *course* they did, Jory thought. And soon he or Kit would have to sneeze, because that's the way it always went in books.

But nobody sneezed, and they made it outside without waking Mom or Ansel.

Everything felt different as they hurried onto the road. The bright afternoon light. The puffy clouds, which only made the blue sky seem bluer.

Jory led the way, with Kit's hand in his. *Gripping* his. "You're pretty strong," he said. "You're going to squish my bones into oatmeal."

She didn't reply. Her eyes darted around like a frightened animal's, and her mouth was a thin line. Usually she was so bold, taunting the blackbirds and dancing in the fields. Jory hoped he hadn't made the wrong decision, leading her out here.

But once they reached the eucalyptus grove, her grip loosened. Then it fell away altogether. She tipped her head back, looking up. The trees made patterns of light and dark on her smiling face.

"Breathe deep," Jory said. "That's eucalyptus. In Australia, koalas eat the leaves."

Kit leaned over and picked up a leaf. She twirled it in front of her eyes, then licked it.

"Kit!" Jory laughed.

"Where are we going?" she asked.

"Just a few more blocks." He pointed. "I want you to meet Alice Brooks-Diaz. From school. You know, the one who asked if our house is haunted."

Kit's smile started to fade.

"She was kidding," he added. "Promise. She's just— she's super interested in things. In everything, but especially mysteries. It used to annoy me, but now that I've gotten to know her, I think she's a lot of fun. Her parents, too."

They continued through the fragrant grove. Suddenly, Kit shrieked. She grabbed Jory's arm as the black-and-white dog bounded toward them, yapping.

"It's okay!" Jory laughed. "I know this dog. He's nice, I promise." He knelt beside the dog and patted its head. "See?"

But Kit still clung to Jory. Did her memories include dogs? Mean ones? Jory decided not to push it—maybe next time.

"Stay," Jory ordered. For once, the dog listened.

—

Alice was waiting on the corner of Vale Street, just like they'd planned. As soon as she saw Jory, she jogged over.

"Oh my gosh! Is that her? Is that really her?" She beamed at Kit. "It's so wonderful to finally meet you, Jory's little sister! Wow, your eyes are like bowling balls. They're gigantic."

Kit's eyes grew even larger. Her hand crept back into Jory's.

"How old are you?" Alice asked.

Jory watched Kit uncertainly. She didn't reply. Which wasn't a surprise—she'd only just started talking, after all. Plus, Alice was a lot to handle, even for him. Maybe they should have stayed in the eucalyptus grove.

"She's almost nine," he said.

"Can't you speak for yourself?" Alice teased Kit.

"Kit doesn't really . . ." Jory felt helpless. "She's . . ."

Alice's grin faltered only for a second. "Okay," she said. "Well, I'm almost twelve. Which makes me three years older than you. Older doesn't necessarily mean wiser, though. Just ask your brother."

"Hey," Jory protested. Kit smiled tentatively.

"So what're we doing today?" Alice shoved back her cuffs. "We've got an hour till I have to be home for dinner. I'd invite you both, but Dad's making kebabs and since he has to, like, craft them, he'd need more notice. They're chicken. Isn't that funny? Mom's over her meatless thing, just like I said she'd be. Although she did manage three days this time."

Jory caught Kit looking at him questioningly. "Kebabs are . . ." he began, then realized he wasn't sure himself.

"Food on sticks," Alice explained. "Like . . . stabbed meat. So you guys don't have bikes, do you? I just got a new one."

Jory shook his head. He'd intended to repair his old bicycle for Kit, but he didn't know how, and Caleb never had time to help.

"Well, we could take a walk, or a hike. Or! We could hit the slopes." Alice grinned at Kit. "I'll bet you'd like them. They're these really fun slides—"

"They're these crazy steep slides on a hillside," Jory interrupted. Not that he didn't love the slopes, but they were way too intense for Kit's first outing. "Super dangerous. I heard about this one kid who slipped and broke every bone in his body."

Alice raised an eyebrow. "What kid?"

"Anyway, they're dangerous," Jory said.

Kit and Alice rolled their eyes at the same time.

"But I'll take you some other day! I promise." He smiled at Kit. "I'll take you everywhere."

She still didn't speak, but she grinned back at him.

"How about we just go to the park?" Alice suggested. "The one a couple blocks away? It's not as good as the one they're building at the new housing development—maybe a six out of ten?—but there are swings, and the normal kinds of slides . . ."

"Great idea." Jory couldn't remember the last time he'd visited a park. Before Mom married Caleb, probably. Which meant he'd never visited one with Kit.

Had she ever been to a park at all?

—

Kit loved it. The monkey bars, the merry-go-round, the slide, the swings. She zipped around like a squirrel drunk on acorns, squealing, laughing. At first, Jory and Alice joined her. But Kit's energy was endless—and exhausting. Finally, they sat together on a bench, watching her play.

"Oh, to be nine again." Alice shoved back her cuffs. "So what's her deal, anyway?"

"Her deal?" Jory repeated.

"The deal with Kit, I mean."

Jory watched as Kit skipped past. Her dark hair stuck up in sixteen different directions. Though he couldn't see them from here, he knew she'd gnawed her nails to the quick. Her ballet slippers were a total disaster—he couldn't believe he'd let her wear them.

He glanced at Alice. Her plaid coat was bright and cheerful, her koala hair neatly bound. Mom would have called her "put together." If Jory hadn't seen her rocket down the slopes, whooping like a night terror, he'd have found her intimidating.

The way he used to.

But Kit—well, Kit was definitely not put together. She looked like a kid who spent too many nights in the bottom of a canyon.

"I just mean, you guys look so different," Alice continued. "Is she your stepsister or something?"

"Oh," Jory said. "No, she's . . ."

Jory turned back to Kit, as she climbed on the swing and started to pump her legs. She swung higher and higher, her hair trailing behind her. Her *dark* hair. Her olive skin. Her big brown eyes that weren't hazel at all, not even in a certain light. He hadn't wanted to believe it, but he knew. He'd always known.

Of course he and Kit weren't related. Not by blood.

"Something like that," he finished.

"And she doesn't talk?"

Jory paused, then shook his head.

"Don't you think that's kind of strange? I mean, my mom gets worried when I give her the silent treatment longer than fifteen minutes."

"You can last fifteen minutes without talking?"

Alice pushed him. "I'm just *saying*—has she been to a doctor?"

"I don't—I don't think so."

"Has she ever said a word?"

"I . . ." Jory didn't know which was stranger: to claim she'd never spoken, or to admit she'd only spoken to him. It was strange either way. Whatever he did, whatever he said, Kit was strange. Her whole story, or lack of one.

"Sometimes I think she fell out of the sky," he said.

A joke. That's what he meant it to be, but it thudded onto the ground between them. Because it wasn't really a joke. Because if things like that were possible, he'd have believed it. It's not like Jory had a better explanation—about Kit, about digging, about *anything*. Until Caleb decided to give him one, Jory had no way to tell between *what if* and *what was*.

"Not aliens again!" Alice said.

Jory shook his head and looked away. He was *tired* of not knowing the answers to her questions. *Tired* of feeling stupid. *Tired* of all the secrets.

Caleb had taught him to look deeper. To think outside the box. To take everything with a grain of salt.

Everything *else*, that is.

When it came to Caleb's orders, Jory wasn't supposed to question. He was supposed to believe there was a reason for everything they did. And why? Because Caleb was family? Because Caleb had saved them?

That's what Mom always said. But Jory was never clear on from *what*. He and Mom had survived just fine on their own.

Alice tapped Jory's shoulder, interrupting his thoughts. "Um, your sister's swinging really high," she said.

Kit was soaring now. Higher than he'd ever seen anybody swing.

"Hey, Kit!" he called, standing. "Take it easy, all right?"

"I don't think she heard you." Alice frowned. "Do you think it's possible to swing all the way over the bar? I thought that was an urban legend, or a suburban legend or whatever, but—wow, she's really pushing it, isn't she . . ."

Jory hurried to the swings. "Kit!" He ducked as her feet whooshed past his head. "That's enough. I'm serious."

She zoomed by him, back and forth, her legs pumping the air, like she intended to launch herself into the sky. Her laughter almost sounded taunting.

"Kit, you're scaring me!"

Finally, she stopped pumping. The swing slowed. Jory waited until her arcs were normal, and then he started for the bench, his heart still thudding in his chest. "Little sisters," he said, trying to sound nonchalant. "They—"

Alice shrieked. Jory whirled back around right as Kit hit the ground.

"Kit!" He ran to her, his heart in his throat.

But she was already getting to her feet, so at least her legs weren't broken. She'd scraped her knees, though. And the elastic on her right ballet slipper had snapped.

When Kit saw her slipper, she started to cry. Silently, the way she always had.

"It's okay," Jory said. "We'll fix it." He turned to Alice. "I should take her home. She wasn't supposed to be playing—it's my fault."

"Why? Is she sick or something?"

"Something like that." Another nonanswer.

"But you can't just . . . Look! She's bleeding!"

Jory looked. Blood leaked from Kit's scraped knees, striping her shins.

"My house is right over there," Alice said. "My mom can fix her up."

Jory shook his head. He couldn't explain that Kit was supposed to be a secret. "We need to go home. Come on, Kit."

He tried to pick her up: first by slinging her over his shoulder, and then with his arms under her knees and waist. He staggered three steps before he almost dropped her. He felt like crying himself—he couldn't carry her all the way home. It was too far. She was too heavy.

"You're being unreasonable," Alice said, stamping her foot. "Why can't you just bring her over for a minute?"

Jory ignored her. "Kit, you've got to walk. Can you walk?"

Kit nodded. The tears in her eyelashes sparkled.

Hand in hand, they hobbled away. Jory refused to look

back, even though he knew Alice was still standing there, watching them go. Now she really would think he was crazy. Because of course it made sense, letting Alice's mother fix up Kit's knees.

Or it would make sense for anybody else. For any other family but Jory's.

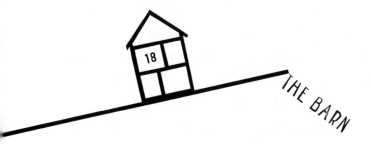

18

THE BARN

CALEB'S TRUCK WAS STILL MISSING, WHICH WAS A RELIEF. But as Jory and Kit crept across the yard, Mom threw open the back door. Concern creased her face, and she clutched her left temple.

"I can explain—" Jory began.

She pushed him aside and knelt in front of Kit. "Honey, you're bleeding!" Mom glanced up at Jory. "What happened? Wait—let's go inside. Keep it down."

"Caleb's at work, right?

"He could be back any minute." She ushered Kit inside, her arm curved protectively around her narrow shoulders. Jory shut the door and locked it.

In the bathroom, Mom helped Kit step into the tub. She rinsed the blood from her knees. The scrapes weren't as bad as Jory had feared, but they still looked raw and painful.

"Now tell me," Mom said. "Where were you? How did Kit get hurt?"

"She tripped and fell. We were playing in the fields—"

"You weren't in the fields. I searched for you all over." She looked at Jory accusingly. "I even searched the canyon."

"You searched the canyon?"

She nodded. "I was so worried about you."

"I'm—I'm sorry." Jory didn't want to lie. But he couldn't tell the truth. Not the whole truth—that he'd brought Kit to meet Alice Brooks-Diaz. That would only worry Mom more, and she was worried enough already. "We just . . . we went for a walk. But Kit fell. That part's real."

"You didn't have permission." Mom helped Kit from the tub, stroking her hair. "What if someone had seen her? We can't let anyone know she's here."

"But . . . the neighbor ladies see her all the time."

"The neighbor ladies?"

"When we play in the fields. They even wave sometimes."

Mom sighed. "They're harmless, I think. But not everybody is, Jory. You don't know who you can trust and who you can't."

Jory sighed, too.

"I just don't understand what you were thinking. You know how upset Caleb will be when he finds out."

Jory's throat closed up. "But—you don't have to tell him, do you?"

"Of course I do! I don't keep secrets from your step-father. And neither should you."

"Then why does he keep so many secrets from us?"

Mom took a deep, shaky breath.

"For our *safety*," she said. "Caleb will tell us everything as soon as it's safe. You know that."

There's only so many times you can hear something before it becomes nonsensical. Like the word *nectarine*. Or the nursery rhyme "Mary, Mary Quite Contrary," with its garden of silver bells.

Jory had heard Caleb's promise a thousand times by now. It was starting to sound meaningless.

—

Jory had heaps of homework. He'd only just started his paper on tunnels. But he couldn't bear to sit around the farmhouse, waiting for Caleb to arrive, while the rest of the family slept.

He headed outside again. The fields didn't feel comfortable either. And he couldn't even look at the canyon without counting the hours until he'd be inside it, snipping, untangling, digging in the ever-expanding darkness.

At the edge of the road, Jory opened the mailbox and peered inside. Nothing. But instead of turning back, he kept walking.

Not toward town—away from it.

The road veered south, through low hills the colors of autumn. After a few minutes, Jory reached another farmhouse. It was painted blue: a cheerful color, like a robin's egg. But otherwise, it was a twin of his family's. It made him feel strange, thinking of the people who lived there.

A family like his, maybe. But different.

Their Kit would have light brown hair, while their Jory and Ansel would be dark. The black-and-white dog would be brown and white, and it would belong to them, not their neighbors. Their family's milk would always be fresh, not powdered. Pickles would be forbidden.

Jory sighed and kept walking.

He walked farther than he'd walked before. As he trudged up a slope, he thought he heard the highway: a low rumbly-rushing sound he felt in his chest. It might be just over the crest of the hill. It probably led to the city—Mom's city. He wondered how long he'd have to walk to get there. If anybody would stop him.

His footsteps slowed.

Then he turned and headed for home.

——

The sun began to set as Jory reached the family's property. Everything was tinted pink. The farmhouse, the fields, the canyon, the barn.

The barn.

From a distance, it appeared ruddy gray, even in the light of the sunset. As he approached, the colors dissolved into flakes and patches, like an Impressionist painting.

Jory remembered how he and Kit used to peel off leaves of paint and save the prettiest ones. Mom had caught them once and made them stop. "Old paint is poison," she'd told them. "It has minerals that seep into your bones. The barn's full of it, Caleb says."

"Poison?"

"And junk. Poison junk. Stay far away from it."

So Jory had. Even if heartbeats under the floorboards and chalk-white faces weren't real, plenty of real-life dangers might hide in the barn. Like snakes. Black widow spiders hunched in the crevices. He'd read a black widow bite could kill a forty-pound child. Though probably not a grown man, like Caleb.

What *kind* of work did Caleb do in here?

Jory's old broken bike leaned against the wall, right where he'd left it. He frowned at it, then headed around to the front.

The barn door was bound by the heavy Jacob Marley chain. When he touched the metal, rust came away on his fingertips. The windows were high up and milky white, like eyes with cataracts. Jory doubted he could see inside, even if he managed to drag a ladder to the barn without anybody noticing.

He stuck his fingers in the crack of the door and tugged.

Then he pulled. The door opened a couple of inches.

When he let go, it shut again.

He wedged his fingers deeper into the crack and tugged harder. The door opened three inches, four, then wouldn't go any farther. But the crack was pretty wide. Maybe . . .

He stepped closer and peeked inside.

It took a moment for his eyes to adjust to the dark confusion. The barn was full of stuff. Not junky stuff, poison or otherwise. Organized stuff. *On purpose* stuff. Boxes. Bins. Plastic tubs with masking tape labels, stacked all the way to the ceiling.

Jory squinted until he could make out a label on the closest bin:

FLASHLIGHTS, LANTERNS

A bin of lights? What in the world for? More digging? With a start, he recognized the handwriting—it wasn't Caleb's. It was Mom's.

Had she been in the barn, too?

Jory's arm muscles ached, but he didn't want to let go. Then he heard a twig snap behind him. He lost his grip on the door and it shut, almost crunching his fingers.

"Looks like we need to have a talk," Caleb said.

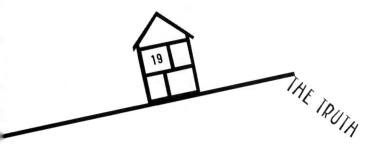

19

THE TRUTH

CALEB STUCK A KEY IN THE PADLOCK. Tiny wisps of rust floated away as the chain fell with a heavy *thunk*—the same *thunk* Jory had heard from his room late at night. The barn door creaked open.

"There's not much light in here," Caleb told Jory, tugging a string. A weak glow filled the crowded space. He switched on a flashlight, then handed it to Jory. "Go ahead and look around."

"Really?" Jory glanced back fearfully, but Caleb didn't look angry. It was hard to tell, though, with so much beard.

"Go on."

Jory crept onto the threshold and aimed his flashlight inside. Bright blue plastic drums took up the most room. They had screw-top lids and spigots. The rest of the space was filled with plastic tubs and buckets and boxes, lining the walls and several long rows of shelves.

BATTERIES: AA, AAA, D, 9-VOLT
SLEEPING BAGS AND BLANKETS
TOILETRIES AND FIRST-AID

Labeled. Purposeful. Organized, saved, and stacked. Caleb must have been stocking the barn for weeks. For *months*, even. And Mom, too, Jory thought unhappily as he scanned more labels she'd written.

KITCHEN: UTENSILS, POTS, SKILLETS
EMERGENCY: MYLAR, FLARES
DEFENSE

Defense? From *what?*

What was all this *for?*

Jory aimed his flashlight down a row. He'd wondered where Mom's preserves had gone. Now, here they were: hundreds of jars or more, filled with the careful remains of the family's harvest. Including pickles. An entire shelf of pickles. Jory couldn't imagine eating them all, even if he ate a pickle every day for the rest of his life.

In the next row, he found tubs with their names.

KIT
ANSEL
JORY

His name. In Mom's handwriting, like all the others. But this one struck him the hardest.

"You can take a look, if you want," Caleb said.

Hesitantly, Jory peeled back the lid of the JORY tub. He aimed his flashlight inside, fearing what he'd find.

". . . Underwear?"

"And socks," Caleb added. "And other clothing. But yes, underwear. The normal kind, and also long. Extra insulated. We don't know how cold it'll get down there."

Jory stared at him. Down there?

Down there.

The sick feeling began in Jory's chest. It spread into his stomach, his arms and legs, every single finger and toe.

Because he knew. *Down there*, underground, beneath the surface of the earth. In the hole they were digging nightly. A giant hole in the ground that wasn't for finding things, or hiding things.

It was a hole for hiding *them*.

—

"So we're digging a bunker," Jory said.

They'd carried the pair of Adirondack chairs to the edge of the canyon. The sun had vanished, and the pink sky had deepened to blue-violet.

"A shelter," Caleb said.

Jory opened his mouth. But for once, he had no questions. Fear and confusion took up too much room. He clasped his hands in his lap so they wouldn't shake.

Shelter.

Bunker.

Down there.

"I remember when I found this farmhouse," Caleb said. "Listed online, among all the other houses for sale. It didn't look like much in the pictures. Run-down, although I knew I could repair it. Nothing in the fields but rotting pumpkins. But I had my heart set on this area: city to the west, desert to the east. Not isolated, but just secluded enough.

"The moment I took a walk out here—the moment I saw the farmhouse and the barn and the canyon and the fields in real life—I knew. That it would be a safe place for us. For me and my family, someday. No matter what happened."

Caleb looked over at Jory. His eyes were grave. "Do you trust me?"

"I . . ." Jory trailed off.

It was a question Caleb had asked countless times. Usually, Jory said yes without thinking.

This time, he thought.

He'd always known Caleb had secrets. Secrets from Jory. Secrets from Kit. Secrets from the rest of the world. But *this*? This was a secret larger than Jory ever could have imagined. Larger, and more terrifying.

And what if it was just the beginning?

What else might Caleb be keeping from Jory?

"I just . . ." Jory tried to keep his voice from trembling. "How long has Mom known? About the—about the shelter?"

He'd almost said bunker again. He wasn't sure where he'd gotten the word—probably when he was researching tunnels online. It was an angled word. An *angry* word. One that made him think of wars and bombs that blotted out the sun. Toxic gas and clouds filled with invisible poison. Alien spaceships clogging the sky.

"A long time," Caleb replied. "Ever since last year, around when you started school again."

Is that one of the reasons they'd sent him back to school? To get him out of their hair while they made preparations? "Does Kit know?" Jory asked.

"We haven't told her anything. Though even if we had, it's not like she'd be able to tell anyone." Caleb smirked with his eyes.

Jory looked away. Kit still hadn't spoken to anyone other than him. "But . . . why didn't you tell *me*?" he asked.

"It wasn't the right time. But now it is. I'm going to tell you the truth."

All of a sudden, Jory wanted to smash his face into the crook of Mom's arm, the way Ansel did. Except Mom was sleeping. Night was looming.

And the answers he wanted—the answers he needed—were right here.

"All right," Jory said nervously.

"When I was a soldier," Caleb began, "the superior officers didn't tell us much. Innocence encourages trust, and trust breeds obedience. With knowledge, however, come questions. As I'm sure you've begun to discover."

But I've always had questions, Jory thought.

"I know you remember the story about the enemy ambush in the alley," Caleb went on. "When my superior officer ordered me to *stay and fight*—but I hid, and he was killed, along with all the others?"

Jory nodded.

"I never told you, but the story didn't end there. The surviving officers jailed me. Because I hid instead of fought, because I valued my own life, they put me behind bars. For almost two weeks. They mocked me and laughed at me. They spit in my food."

Jory felt a fierce rush of loyalty. "They didn't!"

"They did. They treated me like trash—when they remembered I was there. Fortunately, most of the time they forgot about me. They spoke candidly. As if they were alone. And I listened."

"What did they talk about?"

"The enemy," Caleb said.

Jory swallowed. "The enemy you were fighting in the war?"

"Yes, they spoke of that enemy. But not only that enemy. They also spoke of an enemy in the sky."

"The sky," Jory repeated. "Like . . . in airplanes?"

"Maybe," Caleb said.

Jory glanced upward. A cloudless dark had fallen, and the stars shone. He remembered his talk with Alice and shivered. "You're not talking about . . . about . . ." *Aliens*, he thought, but he couldn't make himself say the word.

"All I know is there are enemies. I've been seeking information about them ever since—books, underground publications, radio programs. Every one of them agrees. The enemies are real. And they're everywhere. Above us. Around us. On every side—even our own side."

Jory hadn't thought anything could sound worse than aliens. But this did. "On our own side? Like . . . like who?"

"Government Officials," he said. "Superior officers. Anybody in a position of power. The higher up, the deeper the evil goes.

"Officials don't care who's underfoot when they stomp around, fighting battles and wars over prideful nonsense. There are always wars, and always enemies. And they're not only enemies to each other, but also to the common man. To kids and their parents. To families. To you and me, and to your mother and brother. And to Kit, too—especially to Kit."

Caleb looked at Jory meaningfully.

"Mom already told you?" Jory asked in a small voice.

"She said you took Kit for a walk, and she tripped and fell in the road."

"I was only trying to show her . . ." Jory began, then shook his head. No excuse would be good enough now. At least he hadn't told Mom the whole truth, about Alice and the swings. "I'm sorry," he finished.

"That was stupid, Jory. Stupid, and dangerous. Of both of you."

"It wasn't Kit's idea."

"Only because she never has any," Caleb said, which made Jory frown. "She still knows better—you both do. You never know who might have seen her. And how that might have affected the safety of our whole family."

Jory thought of Alice again. Tugging on her shoelaces. Shoving back her cuffs. Talking about stardust and existential crises, which he still didn't entirely understand. "But . . . not everybody's a danger."

"No, not everybody. Most people aren't. But the problem is, we don't know who from who. Officers don't always wear uniforms. Officials don't always wear suits. The enemy isn't everybody—but it could be *anybody*.

"That's why I've taught you to trust no one. If you assume every person you meet might be dangerous, that they might want to put your life in jeopardy—then they'll never surprise you. There can never be a surprise attack."

"There's going to be an *attack*?"

"I'm sure of it. Any day now. The signs are unmistakable."

The fear spun in Jory's chest again, spiraling into his

throat. He squeezed the arms of his Adirondack chair.

"What are we going to do?"

"What we're doing already." Caleb swept his hand across the canyon. "Look how far we've gotten, Jory! Think about what we're creating. A place for us to stay safe, no matter what happens on the outside. Where we can take care of ourselves, for as long as it takes."

"How long will we be down there?"

"Not very long."

For the first time since they sat down, a tiny spark of hope flickered to life in Jory's middle. "But how long, exactly?"

"We're planning on three months."

The spark died in a blot of darkness. Three months. *Three months in that hole.* Jory had been hoping for a few days. A week at most.

He didn't realize he was holding his breath until Caleb whacked his back. "Breathe," he said. "Breathe. I don't want you to worry—we're going to be fine. We'll make sure the shelter's comfortable. It'll feel just like home. And our stay there will pass much more quickly than you think, I promise."

"But—but if there's really a . . . if there's really an attack . . ." Jory took a deep breath. "What will the world look like when we come out again? How bad will it be?"

"Not bad," Caleb said. "Better."

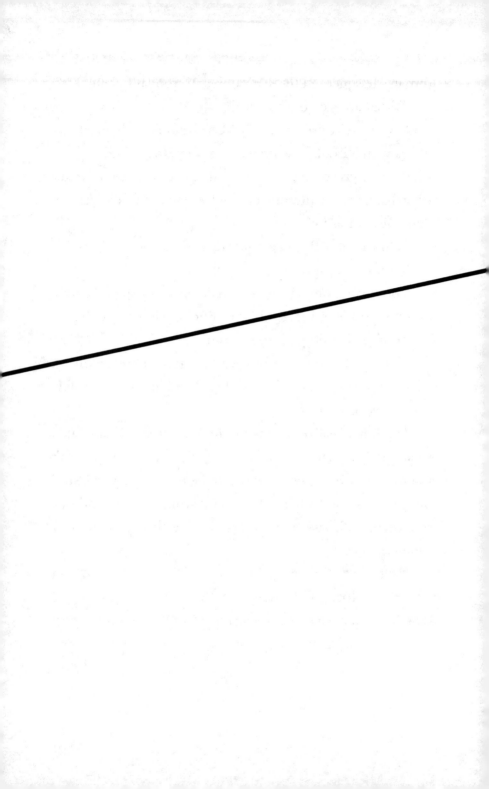

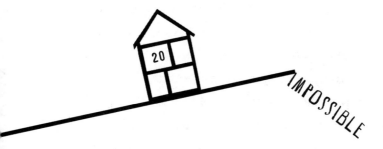

EVERYTHING SEEMED DIFFERENT NOW THAT JORY KNEW.

What.

And why.

But he couldn't think about *why* too long. The thoughts came with too many question marks. Dark, ominous ones that seemed to hover above him. For now, he decided to keep his eyes on the ground. To concentrate on digging.

And digging.

And digging.

Digging with a purpose.

As Jory steered an empty wheelbarrow through the tunnel's opening, he thought again of the tunnels he'd researched online for his social studies project. Basements and cellars. Subways and sewers. Entire villages burrowed in the earth, where people lived by choice.

But those people used bulldozers and dynamite. They didn't even call it digging—they called it excavation. And even in the times before bulldozers and dynamite were invented, people dug in teams of dozens, hundreds, or thousands. Never, ever in teams of five.

Make that four, since Ansel didn't count.

"Ten scoops today," Mom had told him.

He'd scooped up small mounds of dirt with his red plastic shovel, counting loudly. "Fee," he'd yelled. "Faw." When he'd gotten to ten, she'd helped him into another empty wheelbarrow so he could sleep, his grimy hands tucked under his chin.

Jory shook his head. Every time he stepped inside the tunnel, ducking and squeezing to fit, stooping along until it widened into the main space, he thought: *impossible.* Impossible to turn this lopsided, suffocating cave into a bunker—a shelter—that could contain them comfortably. The family and all that stuff in the barn.

Let alone a place that would *feel like home.*

Alone underground, Jory leaned against his half-filled wheelbarrow, inhaling the damp, earthy air through his bandana. Tall stacks of two-by-fours sat in the space's center. He'd helped Caleb carry them down just last week. Beside the stacks, there were heaps of stones Kit had sorted. Flat stones, round stones. Big stones, small stones. Neither of them had known their purpose, or asked. They'd just followed Caleb's orders, like always.

Like the whole time they'd been digging this giant hole—which actually wasn't that giant, when Jory thought about it. Not like the tunnels he'd read about. Or the bunkers.

Was it really *that* much safer down here?

Jory jammed his shovel into a corner and scooped up another pile of dirt. Then he heard a scuffle in the tunnel and paused, letting the dirt slide back into the earth. He aimed his flashlight and found Kit.

"Hey," he said.

She wiggled her fingers in reply. Jory had told her about the bunker earlier that evening, but he wasn't sure if she quite understood. Or if she'd already known.

In the dim light, she looked skinnier than ever. He had no idea how she carried her enormous shovel, let alone dug with it. But that night, just like every night, she never seemed to tire. Despite her bandaged knees—which *had* to be sore—she worked at the same rate as always. While Jory always felt he couldn't bear to dig another shovelful. Now, more than ever.

"Onward and downward," he said.

As Jory pushed the wheelbarrow into the night, he had another realization: *if we never finish the bunker, we'll never have to use it.*

For an instant, he felt hopeful.

But then he saw Caleb. Standing a few yards up the slope, a pickax in his soldier's hands. Jory saw his eyes, pockets of dark under his hooded brows. His broad shoulders, not slopey in the slightest. The way he stabbed his pickax into the earth with gusto, with urgency. With *fury*.

Caleb believed.

He believed everything he said.

As deeply as anyone could believe anything.

———

When Jory thought back over the nights his family had spent in the canyon bottom, each seemed like the night before. They piled up like a heap of stones and dirt, innumerable and endless. Until the night they broke into the water main.

That's when everything *really* began to change.

Instead of leading the family into the canyon that night, Caleb had gathered them in the patio. "I saw a sign this evening," he said gravely.

Five dead birds, all in a row: two sparrows, a robin, and two blue jays. Just lying there on the road. He had been the only one to see them, though—he'd decided to bury the birds without waking the family.

"But the meaning was clear," Caleb said. "The time is drawing near. We need to make sure all our plans are rock solid. All our preparations are concrete. All possible emergencies are accounted for. And that means ensuring we have enough water—by diverting water from the city's pipes."

"Is it really necessary?" Mom asked, twisting her

fingers fretfully. "Aren't we bringing our own water into the shelter?"

"We'll bring drinking water. But need water for many other things—washing, cooking, sanitation. And emergencies. It's better to have too much water than not enough." He turned to Jory. "I want you to come with me."

"Are you sure you don't want me to come?" Mom asked.

"It's a man's job," Caleb said. "Plus, I need you here to watch Ansel. And to turn on the light."

"Turn *on* the light?"

"When I cut into the pipe, it will be loud. As soon as you hear the sound, switch on the lamp. Two, three lamps. And open the blinds. That way, the neighbors think we're all at home, startled awake by the sound."

Mom nodded, her lips tight.

"Now, let's—"

Then Caleb paused, seeming to notice Kit for the first time. She stood beside Ansel, holding his hand. His tawny head rested against her side, his free fingers in his mouth.

"What are you looking at?" Caleb asked her.

Kit blinked at him impassively, even a little defiantly.

"Run along to your room," he said, waving a hand at her. "You're not needed. Jory, let's go."

Before they hiked into the canyon, Caleb showed Jory the plans. "I'll turn off the water main here." He pointed. "It leads to all the pipes in this branch of the canyon."

Jory chewed his lip. "You can just . . . turn it off?"

Caleb nodded. "With pliers. I've done it once before—just to check."

A chaos of pipes covered the paper. Like the snarled roots their shovels uncovered. *So many pipes.* How could Caleb possibly know which water main led to which one?

"But what if the water doesn't shut off?" Jory asked. "What would happen when you cut into the pipe?"

"Well, there would be a flood. It'd be a disaster. But I've studied these diagrams long and hard. You'll have to trust me, son."

—

Trust. Jory tried to hang on to it—*trust* in one hand, *son* in the other—even after he glimpsed the chain saw. Almost as tall as Kit, with black teeth as long as Jory's fingers. Caleb leaned it against a scrub oak beside the uncovered length of pipe, right where he planned to cut. He left to turn off the water main. Jory waited, shivering, the night wind plucking at his jacket.

He realized he'd never been in the canyon alone.

It was *spooky.*

He couldn't see the bunker from here. But it wasn't far. He wondered what would happen to it if Caleb had chosen the wrong water main. If the canyon flooded. Sure, he'd studied the diagrams long and hard. But how could he *know?* And even if it all worked out, wasn't this the sort of thing a person could get in major trouble for?

He was still feeling conflicted when Caleb reappeared, his massive form hulking through the dark. "There's no way to do this quietly," Caleb said, carrying the chain saw to the pipe. "We'll have to settle for quickly. Are you ready?"

Jory bit his lip and nodded.

The chain saw roared on. Before Jory could even clap his hands over his ears, it met the pipe in a shower of sparks. And the sound! An ear-splitting, metallic screech. Like the scream of a dying robot, or a flock of banshees caught in a propeller. His heart jerked as water burst out—but just one burst. Then a trickle. It soaked into the canyon floor and disappeared.

Caleb sawed off a second slice with another metallic screech. And then it was over. He jammed a T-shaped piece of pipe into the gap, swiveled it off, and secured it. Together, they reburied the pipe, then headed down the canyon to turn the water main back on.

"Now we'll have as much water as we need," Caleb said, clapping Jory on the shoulder. "A limitless supply. We'll be safe—no matter how long we need to stay down there."

Jory swallowed. His ears still echoed with that metal-on-metal scream. "What if the neighbors call the police?"

"If they ask, we'll tell them it was a mountain lion. But they won't bother—the danger's growing close. I can feel it. Officials have bigger things to worry about now."

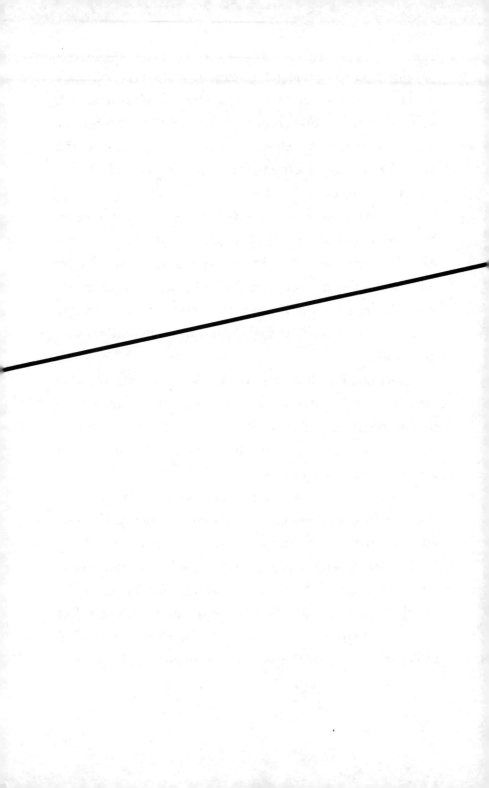

THINGS WERE DIFFERENT AT SCHOOL, TOO. Jory used to have to search for *what ifs*. Now they were everywhere. Battering his head like windblown branches. Swarming his skin like biting flies.

What if nobody else knows about the danger?

What if nobody else is preparing?

What if that's only because nobody's told them?

What if Caleb—

At that, Jory snapped off his thoughts.

He had trouble looking at Mr. Bradley. He had trouble talking to Erik, even when Erik showed him a comic book about a man with a trout for a head. He had the most trouble talking to Alice, especially when she asked about Kit. "How're her knees doing?"

"They're both great," Jory replied.

"So she's okay?"

"She's fine."

Which wasn't really true. But he couldn't talk about how the endless canyon-bottom nights seemed to wear on Kit, about how a kid like her needed the sun. And the sky, any sky—not a roof of stones and dirt. And the stars. If anybody was more than 93 percent stardust, it was Kit.

He couldn't tell Alice that. Or anything on his mind.

So he avoided his friends as much as possible. Sometimes he invented excuses. Mr. Bradley was keeping him after class. He had to stop by the library—*no, that's okay, I study better alone.* At lunch, a series of too-real stomachaches supposedly prevented him from talking.

"You should probably get that checked out," Alice said. "I watched this show on TV about a man who got these terrible stomachaches, and they got worse and worse, and finally he went to the hospital, and it turned out *he had a twin inside* his stomach."

"He ate his twin?" Erik asked incredulously.

Alice nodded. "In the womb."

As Jory crossed the bridge that afternoon, the black-and-white dog bounded up to him, just like he'd hoped. Jory knelt and opened his arms. The dog almost knocked him over backward, even though it weighed thirty pounds, tops. Jory laughed and scratched the dog's ears.

"Panda!"

Jory blinked.

"Panda! Where'd you run off to?"

The dog ducked under Jory's arm and darted away—toward one of the neighbor ladies, who was standing at the end of the bridge. She wore a yellow blouse and cutoff shorts, despite the chill in the air. Her eyes crinkled when she smiled.

"You little rascal," she said, clipping a leash onto the dog's collar.

"He's yours?" Jory asked, even though it was obvious.

"As much as a dog can be anybody's." She walked the dog over to Jory. "He keeps getting out. I mend the fence, he digs right under it. Smartest dog I've ever had."

Jory tried to smile. In his heart of hearts, he'd known the dog wasn't a sign—it was just somebody's dog, like all dogs were. But still, he felt profoundly disappointed. He wouldn't have named the dog Panda, that's for sure. No wonder it kept escaping.

He glanced down. Panda had placed his front paws on Jory's leg.

"He likes you," the neighbor lady said.

"I guess so." Jory knelt to pet him.

"You're Joey, right?"

He nodded.

"Can I ask you a question, Joey? What were you doing in the canyon last night?"

Jory stiffened, his hand freezing in Panda's fur. Had

she seen them climb down? Or back up? Did Mom forget to turn on the lamps? He thought quickly. "Hiking," he said.

"At night?"

"My parents like to take us on nature walks," he said. "To see . . . crickets."

"Crickets?"

"And . . . opossums. And spiders that come out at night—orb weavers." Jory tried to look dangerous. "*Huge* ones. But it's all very educational. We look at the stars, too. My sister Kit, she's a genius when it comes to astronomy. Point out any star, she can name it. Along with all the constellations, galaxies, supernovas . . ." The ease of his storytelling astounded him.

"Kit," the neighbor lady said. "That's your sister's name?"

Oh no. Jory couldn't believe he'd mentioned Kit again! At least in this case, he consoled himself, the neighbor ladies already knew about her. They'd waved. So he hadn't really done anything wrong. Right?

"Um," he replied noncommittally.

"My name's Bonnie. You and your sister should stop by sometime for some scones. I make them with frozen blueberries, so I can whip them up on short notice. You can invite your whole family, if you like."

Jory wasn't sure what a scone was, but his mouth seemed to know. It watered. "Maybe sometime," he said, another lie. He gave Panda one final pat, then turned and trudged away.

—

Day and night and sleeping and waking had gone totally topsy-turvy. Sometimes when Jory zipped on his boots and crept downstairs for a drink of water, he felt startled by the light. Other times he felt like night had taken over entirely. That his hours at school were just a dream, and real life was the bunker in the canyon bottom.

And his dreams. Night infested his dreams, too. Snaky roots and barbed-wire vines. Things he felt but couldn't see in the darkness.

One evening, Jory found Mom sitting at the kitchen table, staring at an untouched plate of toast. It was dark out, but not yet time to dig. Caleb was still at the factory.

"Trouble sleeping?" she asked.

Jory sat across from her. "As usual."

"Me too. I thought I'd have a snack, but . . . I'm just not hungry." She slid the plate a few inches toward Jory. "Do you want some?"

"I'll take half," he said, tearing the bread down the middle. "Any butter?"

"No more butter. We used it up." She picked up her half, then set it down again and sighed. "You'd think I'd have a big appetite, working so hard."

Maybe if Caleb let them buy more butter, Jory thought but didn't say. More butter, or fresh meat, fresh fruit, fresh vegetables. Fresh anything. Caleb thought they should get used to their underground menu, like his soldier MREs, but Jory felt different. Shouldn't they enjoy fresh food while they still had access to it?

"We could go to a restaurant," Jory said. "Next time we run errands . . ."

"Jory," Mom said, a warning.

"I was only joking." He stuffed his mouth with bread.

"I do miss them though." She brushed the crumbs from her fingers. "Restaurants. Not working in them, but eating in them. The way we sometimes used to, before money got so tight."

"Me too."

They sat there quietly, lost in their memories. Mom looking at her hands. Jory looking at Mom. Just the two of them, the way it was before.

Before Ansel. Before Kit.

Before Caleb.

Jory thought about how timid Mom used to be, and how she'd worked in that crummy coffee shop anyway. For them. For Jory—who was her entire family, back then. Which wasn't so timid, was it? Really, it was the opposite. It was brave. A whole lot braver than hiding, no matter what Caleb believed. "I wish you'd told me the truth," Jory said.

Mom looked at him. Solemn, tired-eyed, still pretty. "The truth? You mean . . ."

He nodded. "As soon as you found out."

"I wish I could have," she said. "It was one of the hardest things I've ever had to do. Keeping it from you. But Caleb said the fewer of us who knew, the better."

"How soon is it going to happen?"

"I don't know. Very soon."

"There hasn't been another sign, has there?"

Mom shook her head. "Caleb would have told us."

"Does he tell us about all the signs he sees?"

"Of course. At least the signs he's certain about. The significant ones. Like the newspaper, or the shooting stars, or the birds, or . . ."

"Or anything," Jory finished. "Because a sign can be anything."

Which also meant *anything could be a sign.*

Once the thought had occurred to Jory, he couldn't get it out of his head. How did you know a sign was a sign? How did you *really* know? For sure? If a person wanted to convince somebody something was a sign . . . it might not be that hard.

Depending on how trusting the somebody was.

"Why do *you* believe him?" Jory blurted.

He braced himself for the inevitable scolding. But Mom didn't seem upset with Jory. She sat there in silence for a long, long while. For even longer than last time.

"I don't mean, why do you believe that he wants to take care of us," Jory rushed to explain. "That he cares about us. That *he* believes we're in danger. I just mean—what he says. About the danger. That if we don't seal ourselves up underground . . ."

"I don't know what will happen," Mom said finally.

"You don't?"

"I don't think anybody does," she said. "Not for sure. But I believe Caleb because he believes, with a knowledge and conviction more powerful than any I've ever known. I believe him because he's brilliant, and strong, and I love him, and trust him. Because he's always taken care of us, ever since he saved us—"

"Saved us from *what*?" Jory interrupted.

Mom looked surprised. "What do you mean?"

"I know you hated working at the coffee shop. But weren't we doing okay? Just the two of us?"

"Oh, Jory," Mom said. Her voice grew softer, sadder. "I was barely making enough for us to live on—not even enough. I was two months late on rent for our apartment. We had nobody to help us. No friends, no family. I didn't know any of our neighbors. When I lost my job, if Caleb hadn't been there . . ." Tears shone in her eyes. "I don't think I'd have been able to take care of you anymore."

Jory had no idea things had gotten that bad. Mom must have been so lonely, with nobody to turn to. She must have been so scared.

"So I believe Caleb because I love him," Mom said again. "I do. And because . . ."

She looked at her hands.

"Because . . . what if I don't believe him—and I'm wrong?"

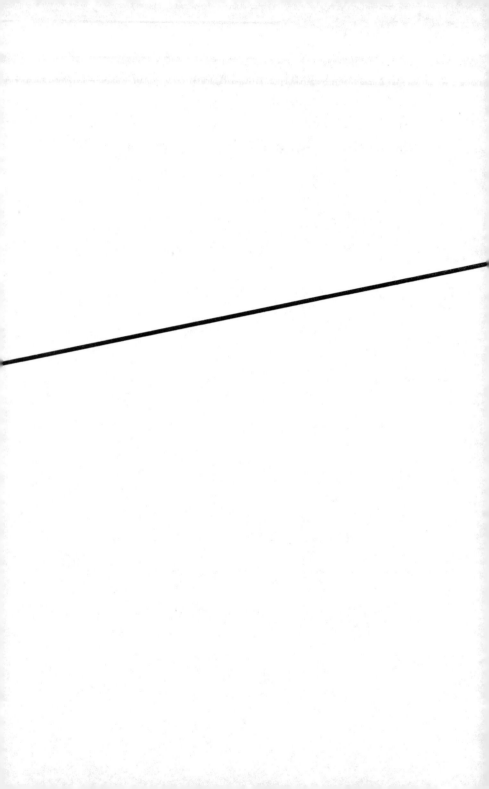

22 FRIENDS

JORY WALKED HOME THE SHORT WAY THAT TUESDAY, his head
down, hands in his pockets. He remembered how old he'd
felt that first week in the canyon. It made him want to laugh.
If he'd felt seventy then, he felt one hundred now. Maybe
older.

He didn't see Panda as he walked across the bridge,
even after he whistled softly. The neighbor ladies must have
repaired their fence.

He'd only just reached the fields when he heard a
voice.

"Wow, nice place!"

Jory's stomach sank into his ankles. *Make it a neighbor,
make it a Boy Scout, make it anybody but them.* He scrunched
up his face, then turned.

Erik Dixon strolled toward him, waving emphatically. Sam Kapur and Randall Loomis walked on either side of him.

A couple of yards back, Alice Brooks-Diaz plodded along with her plaid arms crossed. "I *told* them," she said. "I *told* them it was a jerk move, showing up unannounced, but they wouldn't listen. We were chatting about how it's been ages since we hung out, and Erik got this snail-brained idea to come see you, and I'm sorry Jory, really I am—"

Jory sprinted over to join them. "It's okay," he said, although it wasn't. Even if Jory trusted them, Caleb wouldn't. If he saw them on the family's property? He'd be furious. Good thing he wasn't home yet. "Just . . . keep your voices down."

"Why?" Sam looked around. "There's nobody out here."

"My family's sleeping."

Randall scoffed, adjusting his baseball cap. "But it's, like, four in the afternoon."

"His stepdad works nights," Alice whispered.

"Uh, right," said Jory.

"So let's not piss him off, guys. I know how my dad gets when he gets woken up. He's like a bear with a hive on his head. All growly and stuff."

Jory couldn't imagine Mr. Diaz getting all growly and stuff. "Also, my brother's little, and—"

"I didn't know you had a brother!" Alice exclaimed, then covered her mouth.

He tried not to groan. At least Ansel wasn't supposed to be a secret.

"What about Kit?" she asked. "Is she here? I was hoping to see her—"

"She's busy right now. She's sleeping."

"Which is it?"

"Both. I mean, she's busy sleeping. She's sick. She had a long night—a long day." Jory rubbed his brow. He was letting stuff slip all over the place. "She's very, very sick."

"Oh, jeez! Have you taken her to a doctor?"

"Oh, no—she's not that sick. She'll be fine."

Alice looked at him funny. "Well . . . tell her I said to get well soon."

Erik was swiveling his head from left to right, taking in the family's property. "So are you going to take us on a farm tour, or what?"

"It's not a real farm," Jory said. "I've told you a thousand times. It's not like we've got geese and goats and baby lambs."

"Baby lambs!" Alice squealed.

Jory rolled his eyes. "We don't have any animals. Except this dumb dog that comes around—but only sometimes. We did grow things, but they're all gone now."

"What kind of things?"

"Squash. Whatever. Nothing special . . . Come with me and I'll show you." The farther from the house, the better, Jory supposed.

He led them to the fields. The ground was mostly barren. Brittle vines curled over the dirt, and a few withered pumpkins danced with tiny flies. A rusty rake lay on its side in a garden of rocks.

"*Man,*" Erik said wistfully. "This is all yours? My yard's the size of a postcard. This place is a hundred thousand times bigger than my whole house."

Jory felt proud and embarrassed at the same time. "We've got something even better. Follow me."

The other kids followed, picking their way through the vines. Jory was careful to lead them nowhere near the family's footpath down. He swept one hand across the expanse of open space, as Caleb had. "This is our canyon."

"Wow!" Erik exclaimed.

Sam looked less impressed. "Why *wow*? Our town's got hundreds of these."

"I don't know. Maybe because it's this gigantic chasm in *Jory's own backyard.*" Erik swiped Randall's baseball cap and tossed it to Sam, who pretended to throw it into the canyon. Randall tackled him around the waist. Jory laughed, though he wished they'd lower their voices a little.

"So do you guys actually own all this?" Erik asked him.

Jory wasn't sure. "Part of it, I think."

They crowded as close as they could to the canyon's edge. A hawk swooped overhead, but that was the only danger in today's blue sky. The color, the sunlight, his classmates' jokes . . . they made it seem almost silly now. That anything could possibly threaten them from above.

Or that he'd be spending so much time below.

Suddenly, Jory noticed Bonnie, the neighbor lady he'd spoken to, on the canyon's opposite side. She looked about as big as one of those plastic army men. Small enough to squish with two fingers.

Alice waved at her. She waved back.

Jory caught Alice's hand. "Don't," he said. "She's weird."

"Weird like how?"

"Weird like . . ." Jory tried to look at her without actually looking. "She's old, but she wears short shorts all the time."

Alice laughed. "Why's that weird? I plan on wearing short shorts when I'm old. That's the whole point of being old—you can wear whatever you want. Like go-go boots and a Renaissance neck cuff. Or a wedding dress and a horse mask."

The other boys laughed.

"Fine," Jory said. "But rumor has it, all she and the other neighbor lady eat is—pickles. They only eat pickles. Nothing else. Also, they're building a house in the bottom of the canyon."

Jory wasn't sure why he'd said that—it'd just come out. All five of them stared into the canyon.

"Why in the world?" Erik said. "They've got a perfectly good house right there."

"I don't know," Jory said. "I guess they're just a little crazy."

"No kidding," Sam agreed.

"Probably all the sodium," Alice said.

Randall raised his eyebrows. "The sodium?"

"From the pickles. Those things are loaded."

"Okay, but, for real? They're really building a house down there?" Erik stepped even closer to the edge. A pebble clattered down the slope. "We should go check it out."

Jory was horrified. "Oh no, that's a bad idea."

"Why?"

"Because . . . poison oak! There's tons of it down there. The evil kind. Six hours later you'd be one big oozy blister."

"Doesn't your neighbor tramp around down there in short shorts?" Sam asked.

Oops. "She's probably immune," Jory said. "I read that like one tenth of the population is immune to poison oak and ivy. But the odds are against us. Anyway, there are other things too. Scorpions. Coyotes. Spiders—hairy ones."

Alice shrieked, then started laughing. Erik had tickled the back of her neck. Jory looked away, feeling kind of annoyed.

And then his heart dropped.

Mom was heading toward them.

For a split second, he saw her through the other kids' eyes. Her lopsided, frizzy braid. Her broken-bird frailty. Her pale skin—like she hadn't seen the sun in months.

Then she was Mom again. Frail and frazzled, sure—but worried. Distressed. Even more distressed than when he'd brought Kit home bleeding. Home was home and school was school, but now they were colliding.

Jory cleared his throat. "Hi, Mom. These are my . . . they're kids from my class."

"We're his friends," Alice said.

Jory glanced at her, then swallowed. "They just wanted to see—where I lived."

Mom blinked over and over, like she had something in her eye. "I'm afraid Jory needs to come inside now," she said softly. "It's time for dinner."

"Really? But it's only—"

Alice elbowed Erik in the side before he could finish. "No problem. It's very nice to meet you, Mrs. Birch."

Mom smiled in a strained way. "You, too."

Jory followed her inside the house, battling not to glance back. His stomach swarmed with butterflies, angry hornets, miniature dragons with fiery sighs. He felt upset with everybody—Sam and Randall, Erik and Alice, Mom and especially himself.

But he also felt loyal to them. All of them. His family, but also his friends. It wasn't their fault they didn't know any better. It wasn't their fault they had nobody to warn them of the danger.

His friends.

Alice had used the word herself: *We're his friends*, she'd said. She'd used it other times, too. Did that make it true? Was that how friendship always was? People easing into each other's company bit by bit, until suddenly they cared?

In the kitchen, Mom leaned against the counter with her arms crossed.

"They're not . . ." Jory began. "We weren't . . ."

She watched him, waiting.

He took a deep breath. "They just showed up. They followed me—"

"It's okay."

"And I know you have to tell Caleb—"

Mom touched his arm. "I won't."

Jory gaped. "You won't?"

"Did you tell them anything?"

She didn't specify, but he knew what she meant. "No, of course not."

"Then Caleb doesn't need to know." Mom smiled, almost sadly. "I'm heading for bed—I've got a bit of a head-ache. Will you be all right making your own dinner?"

Jory nodded.

But his stomach dragons had flown off with his appetite. He sat at the kitchen table with his hands in his lap, staring at the blinds that shaded the kitchen window.

He knew he should feel relieved. Even though he hadn't done anything wrong, not really. Mom was right—Caleb didn't need to know. Still, he felt uneasy.

Trust was a fragile thing. So was belief.

And both were starting to crumble.

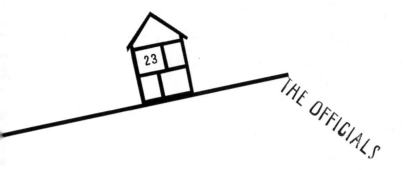

THE OFFICIALS

On Saturday, Jory, Kit, and Ansel sat together at the kitchen table, a mound of Worldbuilding houses between them. They typically played on the back porch or in the fields, but Jory was feeling daring. Mom and Caleb had left early to run errands, and they said they'd be gone all day.

"That's a house," Kit told Ansel, pointing. She was speaking more often now, though still only to her brothers.

"Howf," Ansel repeated.

"Close enough."

Ansel seemed to like Worldbuilding. Kit had given him a block and a brush of his own. So far, he'd painted the whole thing bright yellow, and his hands, too. And his forehead.

"You're a mess, buddy." Jory chuckled, even though knew he'd have to scrub him before Mom and Caleb returned. "You look like Big Bird."

"Bird," Ansel said.

"Exactly right!" Kit exclaimed, and Ansel beamed. "What's Big Bird, anyway?"

Jory glanced at her in surprise. "Oh—I guess you haven't seen *Sesame Street*. He's a great big yellow bird with orange legs. Taller than a man."

"Sounds freaky."

"He's supposed to be friendly," Jory tried to explain.

Rap. Rap. Rap.

He accidentally painted a green splotch over his window.

"The door," Kit said, eyes wide.

He set down his house and rinsed his hands in the sink, trying to act calm. "Stay here. Clean up while I answer it."

Rap. Rap. Rap.

Each knock was a sharp pang of fear in Jory's chest. Should he answer the door? Or should he hide? What would Caleb want him to do? There wasn't enough time to figure it out. He hurried to the door, took a deep breath, and opened it.

Two strangers stood on the other side. Two strangers in trim suits and shiny shoes. White collared shirts. Serious expressions.

Two *Officials*.

"Hello," they said in unison.

The female Official was short and pudgy, with curly hair and glasses. The male Official had cropped gray hair and a sunburst of smile lines around his eyes. Other than the formal clothes, they looked almost *normal*. But looks could be deceiving, Jory knew. He didn't trust them one bit.

"You must be Jory Birch," he said. "Eleven, almost twelve years old, right? Are your parents home?"

"They'll be back soon," Jory said. "I mean, I don't know when they'll be back. You should probably stop by another time."

He started to close the door.

"We'd like to talk to you, then," the male Official said. "If that's all right. Can we come in and chat for a bit?"

Jory shook his head. "That's probably not a good idea. Because of . . ."

"Because of what?"

"Because of serial killers."

They both smiled. Jory didn't like the man's teeth—his canines seemed too sharp. "We're not serial killers," the female Official said, fumbling through her pocket. She held out a badge.

Jory pretended to examine it. PROTECTIVE SERVICES, he read. Very Official-sounding. If the badges were fake, he wouldn't know the difference—and what did it matter? He couldn't trust Officials, even if the badge *was* genuine. "You still can't come inside," he said.

"Fair enough," the female Official said. "If you could just answer a few—"

There was a tug on Jory's jeans. "Jawee," Ansel said.

"Who's this?"

"That's my brother," Jory said grudgingly.

He tried to pat down Ansel's messy hair. Where was Kit? Staying out of sight, he hoped.

"Heya, Buddy-Boy," the male Official said, kneeling down. "You're an awfully cute little fellow. How would you like an Andes mint?"

"He's allergic to chocolate," Jory lied. He wondered whether lying to an Official was a federal offense.

"I've also got some saltwater taffy. Let me check my pockets . . ."

Jory didn't trust any of this man's candy. "We're fine."

"So it's just the five of you?"

"Yeah, the—" Jory stopped. "Mom, me, Caleb and Ansel. And our dog. Five."

"So you don't have a sister?"

"No."

"That's funny. We have reports of a little girl living here. With dark hair, about eight or nine years old, is that right?"

"I told you," Jory said. "I live here. My mother lives here. My stepfather, Caleb, lives here. And Ansel lives here."

"And the little girl."

Jory felt like screaming. "It must have just been my friend Alice Brooks-Diaz. She's got dark hair. Maybe—"

"No, it couldn't be," the male Official said. "It was Alice's mother who called us about your sister in the first place."

Alice's mother had called? Jory felt punched in the gut. How did Mrs. Brooks even *know* about Kit? There was only one possible way—Alice had told her. But why? When? After Kit had fallen from the swing? Or yesterday, after his friends had followed him home? Probably yesterday. She'd looked at him so strangely when he'd said Kit was sick.

He was so stupid! *Alice* was so stupid. She had no idea how dangerous the Officials were. They didn't want to protect Kit, no matter what they said.

He stepped forward. The male Official leaned backward, just a bit.

"I don't know who told you what," Jory said, "but I don't have a sister. There's no little girl living here. There's just me and Ansel and Mom and Caleb."

"And your dog."

Jory wished he hadn't brought the dog into this. "I swear on—on everything in the world. On a stack of holy Bibles. On my mother's grave. All right?"

Finally, the male Official nodded. "All right."

"Everything else is okay?" the female Official asked.

"Everything's fine."

"Remember, Jory, we're here for you. Here's a card with our office's phone number on it. Feel free to call anytime."

Jory shut the door—as politely as possible, even though he wanted to slam it. Then he crumpled the card in his fist.

It was just like Caleb said. The Officials were out to get them. They were out to get *Kit*. And if Caleb was right about the Officials . . .

Maybe he was right about everything else.

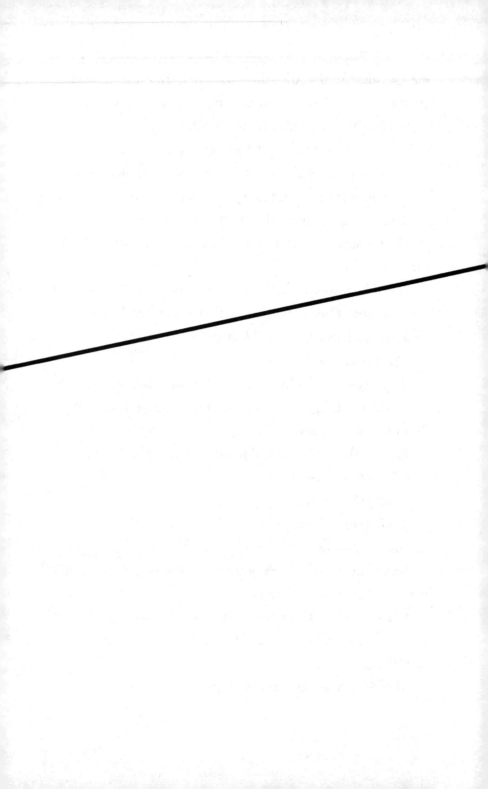

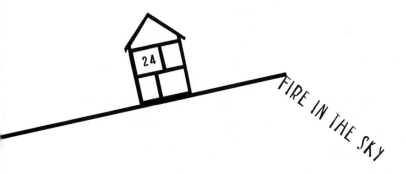

JORY WAITED UNTIL THE REST OF HIS FAMILY HAD FALLEN ASLEEP. Then he found Caleb studying by lantern light in the patio, flipping pages in one of his thick binders. Jory heard the low murmur of the radio—*"not telling you . . . proprietary information . . . coming storm . . ."*—before Caleb reached over and switched it off.

"What's the trouble, son?" Caleb asked.

Nervously, Jory handed him the female Official's crumpled card. Caleb smoothed it with callused fingers as Jory shared what they'd said.

"So they were interested in Kit," Caleb said quietly.

"Yeah, but . . ." Jory hadn't really specified. "How did you know?"

"It was only a matter of time before they learned about her."

"*Why* are they interested in her?"

Caleb shut his binder and sat back in his Adirondack chair. His face was turned away from the lantern light, so Jory couldn't read the expression in his eyes. "Because Kit is special."

Kit is special.

Jory thought about Kit's star-shaped eyes in his dream, that impossible wind. Her fingertip electricity that had ruffled Ansel's hair. He thought about the way she always seemed to know what Jory was thinking. Whether he was awake or asleep. Her creative brilliance, and the energy that crackled through her. Jory didn't know what special meant exactly, but he wasn't surprised.

Of course Kit was special—that was obvious. A girl made of stars. A girl from the moon, magicked into his life—

"I thought so, anyway," Caleb said.

"So she's not special?" Jory asked, confused.

"She seemed to be, at first. When she showed up bedraggled in our pumpkin field, and I saw how happy she made your mother, I took it as a sign. Not a bad sign—a good one. I decided the only right thing to do was to keep her safe: from wherever she came, from whoever might be seeking her. To welcome her into our family, even if that meant keeping her a secret. But I'm afraid I made a mistake."

Jory gaped at his stepdad. "A mistake?"

"The truth is, Kit isn't special—she's just a normal little girl. Subnormal, even. She hasn't spoken or written a word since we found her. She reads, but doesn't retain anything—"

"But she does. I *know* she does."

Caleb sighed, rubbing his beard. "I know you care about her. And Mom does, too. But whether she's special or not, having her in our possession has brought attention to our family. Our *real* family."

Kit is our real family, Jory thought fiercely.

He knew Caleb had never seemed to care for Kit the way Jory and Mom did. And that he seemed more frustrated by her lately. His fuse was shorter, more easily tripped. Like when she'd spilled her milk during Survival. And the night they'd cut into the pipe, when he'd sent her to her room.

But Jory hadn't realized Caleb thought of her this way. Not as a daughter, but somebody who should be grateful for their care. Maybe even somebody who owed them.

"It's getting late," Caleb said. "We have a long night ahead of us. Maybe I'll give the Officials a call first thing in the morning—I'm sure I can divert their attention. For now." He stood and rested a hand on Jory's shoulder. "You were right to approach me in private, son."

"I was?"

Caleb nodded. "I don't think we should tell your mother about the Officials."

It made Jory uncomfortable, this feeling he had knowledge his mother didn't. Especially after she'd kept the secret about his friends. "Why not?"

"She'll worry too much. Your mother has a compassion-ate heart. Sometimes, it makes her weak. When the danger comes, she'll need to rely on our strength—on yours, Jory. On your trust, and your love for this family."

Jory wanted to defend Mom. To insist she was stronger than Caleb thought, stronger than *any* of them thought. She couldn't help her migraines, her timidity, her anxiety—and she looked after the family, despite those extra challenges.

But there it was: *the danger* again. Skulking behind every conversation. Storming his every thought with darkness.

"Can you be strong?" Caleb asked.

"I'm—I'm trying," Jory said truthfully.

"Good." Caleb's eyes smiled. "And don't worry about Kit. When we took her in, we took on the responsibility to make sure she's taken care of. And I intend to."

It didn't make Jory feel much better.

———

Jory tossed and turned that night, though he desperately needed sleep. Every time he started to doze—

Rap. Rap. Rap.

Just his imagination knocking. But every time, he'd sit up in bed, certain the Officials had arrived to take Kit away, to take Ansel away, to take *him* away.

Maybe he was having an existential crisis.

Finally, he kicked off the covers and stuffed his feet in

his boots. He considered taking a stroll in the fields, or maybe seeing if Kit was awake. He hadn't gotten the chance to discuss the Officials with her. It was so difficult, finding time and space for secret talks.

Instead, Jory crossed the room and lifted his blinds. He slid open the window.

No wind blasted him in the face, like on the night he'd dreamed of Kit. He saw the fields, and the blackness of the canyon. The purple-gray sky curved around it, littered with stars.

So many stars.

They flickered at the edge of Jory's vision, stilling when he stared. He wished he had a telescope. Or an astronomy book. Or an astronomy genius, like he'd pretended Kit was to the neighbor lady. He had no idea which lights were stars, satellites, planets. Which were other things. Things he didn't know about. Things he couldn't name.

The sky was endless. And so were the possibilities.

Dangerous possibilities, maybe.

But not *all* of them. Not *every* mystery was a danger—like Mr. Bradley had said. Right?

Jory focused on a reddish star, the brightest light in the sky. Maybe it was Mars—that was the red planet, right? Or was that Jupiter? No, Jupiter had the red spot. For some reason Jupiter had always given him the creeps. As he watched, the light seemed to grow redder, more radiant.

He held his eyes closed for five seconds. When he opened

them, the light hadn't dimmed. It was brighter. Almost sun-bright, now—scary bright.

And *red*.

Red enough to burn, but he couldn't look away. It was so beautiful. But also so *furious*. A fire in the sky. A flaming red eye, staring straight at Jory.

It was a sign.

It *had* to be. A sign for him, because he'd been doubting—and he was sure, almost entirely sure, what it meant.

The danger was real.

But which danger, Jory didn't know.

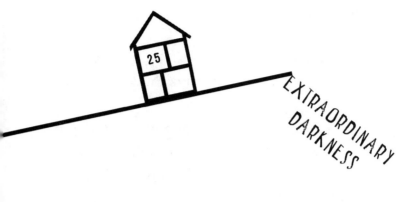

25
EXTRAORDINARY DARKNESS

OUT OF THE CORNER OF HIS EYE, Jory glimpsed a flash of plaid. He sighed. He'd managed to avoid Alice all morning, but at lunch he was a sitting target. He should have found a doghouse to hide inside. Or gone to the nurse with an upset stomach—this time, it wouldn't have been a lie.

"Jory?" Alice said.

He stared at his untouched lunch. I don't want to talk to you, he thought. I have nothing to say to you.

"Do you need a napkin? Or a fork? Or—?"

He didn't reply. He swiveled away, just far enough to make a point.

"What's going on?" She laughed nervously. "Are you giving me the silent treatment? What are you, three? Why are you acting like that?"

Finally, he looked her in the eye. "We can't be friends anymore."

"Excuse me, what?"

"I said, we can't be friends anymore."

Alice stood there with her mouth half open. "You can't just . . . Jory, you can't just say that sort of thing without an explanation."

So she didn't know her mom had contacted the Officials? Well, that didn't make it any less Alice's fault. She'd still told a secret that wasn't hers to share. "Just—go away, all right?" It came out louder than he intended.

"What's going on?" Erik asked, coming over and standing beside Alice.

"Jory says we can't be friends anymore," she said.

"He said *what*?" Erik stared at Jory. "What's your deal?"

Alice's eyes shone. Was she going to cry? Jory couldn't believe it. She should be glad to get rid of him. Her Tuesdays would be free.

"What's wrong with you, man?" Erik said. "You should be happy to have a friend like Alice. You should feel *lucky*."

Jory felt like the entire cafeteria was staring at him. And people outside the cafeteria, too. He felt like everybody in the entire world had turned their heads at that moment, and was staring at him accusingly. Who in their right mind would unfriend Alice Brooks-Diaz?

Erik threw his hands in the air. "You know what? Forget it."

Then the lunch monitor came over. "Is anything wrong?" she asked. "Alice, why are you crying? Were the boys teasing you?"

Jory couldn't take it anymore. "*Nothing's* wrong!" he exclaimed. "Nobody's teasing anybody, and everything is fine. I'm fine. And I'd be even *more* fine if everybody would just *leave me alone.*"

He picked up his lunch tray and threw it. It banged across the cafeteria floor, clattering to a stop near the trash cans.

A tidal wave hush fell over the nearest tables. Now everyone really was staring at him.

"I think you and I should head back to your classroom," the lunch monitor said. "Now."

Jory followed her with his head down, hands in his pockets. He felt rotten. Literally rotten. Like his fingers and toes and arms and legs were hanging dead and floppy from his body. His brain, too, felt rotten inside his head.

He *had* been happy to have a friend like Alice. He *had* felt lucky.

But what did that matter now? He couldn't have *any* friends underground.

Jory sat at his desk while the lunch monitor explained the situation. After she left, Mr. Bradley seated himself at the desk next to Jory's. He had to pretzel his long legs to fit.

"So listen up, buddy," he began. "I'm worried about you.

You've always been reserved, but you've been withdrawing even more lately—until this outburst."

"Sorry," Jory muttered.

"Also, you haven't fully caught up on all that schoolwork you've missed."

"I've been trying."

"I can tell, and I appreciate that. But still, you're getting further and further behind. Is your social studies project almost finished?"

Almost. In fact, Jory had written most of it. But he couldn't finish it.

He couldn't bear to.

He knew plenty about tunnels. More than anybody in the class. More than anybody in the school—even more than the teachers, probably.

Not only did he know about their history—tunnels through time, bunkers and subways and underground villages, vaults and cellars and burial grounds—but he also knew what it was like to dig. He knew what it was like to open up the earth and crawl inside. The extraordinary darkness of a place the sun will never reach.

"Jory? Your essay?"

Jory stared at his hands. He wondered if the black dirt underneath his fingernails was permanent. Or if he'd ever get it all out. Maybe with a heavy-duty scrub brush and industrial-strength nail cleaner. If that existed, after.

"I don't feel like you're listening to me," Mr. Bradley said.

He thought about how dirt came from rocks, and rocks came from mountains. Mountains under his fingernails. And probably stardust, too.

Mr. Bradley sighed. "If you won't talk to me, I'm going to have to call your parents."

Now Jory looked up. "What? But—but you already did."

"We both know you haven't shown much improvement since last time I called. It's for the best. I can ask them to meet with me this week, and maybe together we can come up with a plan to get your studies back where they belong."

Jory imagined Mr. Bradley and Caleb facing off. Even Mr. Bradley, with his towering height and booming voice, would be no match for Caleb's soldier strength. Nobody was. Jory's palms began to sweat. Home was home and school was school and he couldn't *bear* it.

"You can't call my parents again," Jory said. "You *can't*."

"I have to—"

Jory shook his head so hard his brain rattled. "We don't need them! We can come up with a plan without them. And you can punish me any way you want. I'll stay after school every—every Tuesday, for the rest of the year. I'll skip lunch. I'll do anything, just please, *please* don't call my parents."

"Jory, is everything all right at home?"

Jory tried to breathe normally, but it was hard. So hard. "Everything's fine at home! Everything's just great."

"Then why don't you want me to call your parents?"

"Because . . . because . . ." Jory's thoughts raced, stumbled, fell face-first onto the ground. His weary brain couldn't think of an excuse that would make sense.

Mr. Bradley reached into his pocket and pulled out a phone. "How about we talk to them together?" he suggested. "That's a compromise. If you want, you can—"

Jory grabbed the phone.

He ran.

—

Mr. Bradley definitely wouldn't chase him. He was old—compared to Jory, anyway—and more than that, he was a *teacher*. Teachers didn't run. It wouldn't be dignified. It wouldn't be professional.

"Jory! Come back here!"

Mr. Bradley was definitely chasing him.

"Stop right now and give me my phone!"

Jory heard Mr. Bradley's dress shoes clapping on the pavement. Should have worn boots, Jory thought. Much more practical for digging, climbing canyon walls, and racing across the school grounds with stolen technology.

The cafeteria had let everybody out, so the schoolyard was packed with kids. This time, Jory didn't care about their stares. He was a soldier, boots pounding across a desert landscape. He leaped over a pair of third graders cross-legged in the grass and almost plowed into a jungle gym. He ducked under it—and somebody caught his arm.

"What are you doing, young man?" A teacher he didn't recognize squinted into his face.

Mr. Bradley caught up, huffing and puffing. "That wasn't funny. Hand over my phone, right this minute."

"Okay," Jory said, looking contrite. He handed over the phone.

Then he twisted free and ran toward the fence.

A padlock sagged from the gate. But it was nothing like the barn lock. When Jory tugged at it, the gap was just large enough for him to squeeze through.

He sprinted from the schoolyard, past the houses and through the eucalyptus grove, long after he knew Mr. Bradley had stopped chasing. But he knew it was too late. Mr. Bradley would call Caleb, and Caleb would be furious.

Jory had done the worst thing of all—he'd brought even more attention to the family, right when they needed it least.

Hiding is much harder when somebody is seeking.

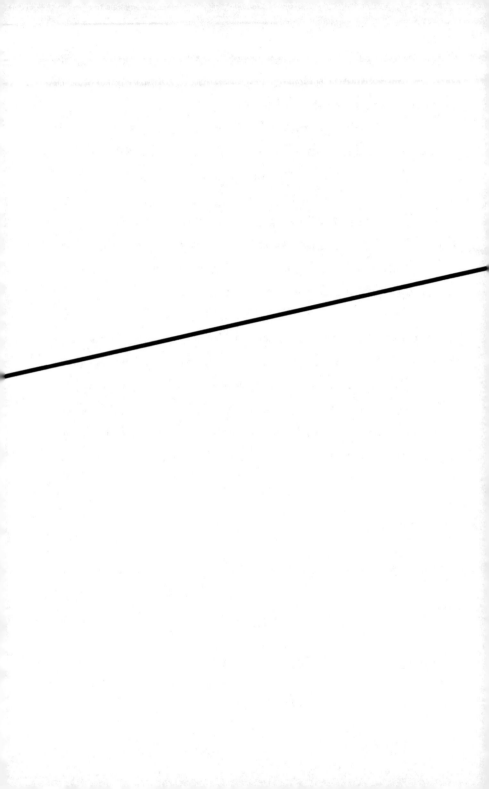

26

TOO LATE

"I CAN'T BELIEVE THAT MAN CHASED YOU," MOM SAID.

"A grown man chasing an eleven-year-old boy. If I'd been there, I would have . . ." Caleb shook his head. "Nobody treats my son like that."

Jory stood up straighter, feeling even more righteous. When he'd arrived home from school two hours early, he'd felt ashamed. He'd almost considered turning right around and running . . . well, running somewhere. The slopes, maybe. He would soar down the slopes at top speed and hope they'd propel him off the face of the earth.

But he made himself open the door. He made himself ask Mom and Caleb to meet with him in the patio, and he made himself tell them the truth—most of it, anyway. And instead of getting angry at him for disobeying Mr. Bradley, they took Jory's side.

They took his side!

That was the best thing about family. They had your back.

"You're so brave." Mom squeezed Jory's shoulder, then shifted Ansel to her other hip. "We know how hard it's been on you, going to school all stooped with secrets."

"So you're not angry at all?" Jory asked.

"Angry, yes," Caleb replied. "But not at you, son. Angry at that house of lies they call a school. That sham they call education."

Jory's shoulders wilted a bit. He liked Caleb standing up for him—but he also liked learning. School was the best place for that.

Brrrrng. Brrrrng.

The phone. Jory gulped. "My teacher wants to meet with you."

"Don't worry." Caleb stood, rubbing his beard. "I'll meet with him tomorrow. I'll tell him we've decided you'll be homeschooled again. We were about to pull you out of school anyway—it'll just happen a few days sooner than we'd planned."

Jory's stomach dragons fluttered awake. As soon as Caleb left, he turned to Mom. "What does he mean, a few days?" he asked fearfully. "Is it that soon?"

She nodded. "You know we're almost finished with the shelter."

"But I didn't think . . . I thought there'd be more time.

I'm not done with school. I haven't learned everything yet. . . ."

Mom reached for Jory's hand, but Caleb reappeared before she could respond. "Is it all taken care of?" she asked him.

"For now," Caleb replied. "We don't need them to believe us for long."

He and Mom locked eyes for just a couple seconds, but it felt like much more passed between them. Jory broke their spell with a question. "Three months, right? You said we'll be in the shelter for three months?"

Caleb nodded. "That's my best estimate."

Jory wondered if three months would be long enough for his classmates to forget. It probably depended on what happened in those three months. "What if we come out after three months," he said, "and it's still dangerous outside? Or if . . . or if we realize we went down there too early? That the danger hasn't even come yet?"

"That won't be a problem," Caleb said.

Jory was afraid to ask his next question. "Why not?"

"We have enough supplies for six months."

———

That night, Jory dreamed that he left his boots at the slopes. The family stood in the fields, dressed and zipped and buckled, ready to go. A high-pitch alarm wailed in the background, like a mosquito scream amplified. Overhead, the stars began to go out, one by one.

Where are your boots, son? Caleb asked.

Jory explained where he'd left them. *I'll go get them right now, it'll just take fifteen minutes, please wait for me. . . .*

Mom hugged Ansel and shook her head sadly. Kit turned her face toward the darkness. The sky grew blacker and blacker—only a few stars were left.

Please, Jory begged.

Sorry, Caleb said. *But it's too late.*

And the last star went out.

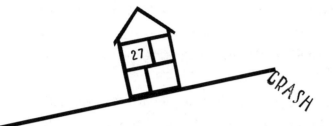

JORY HAD THOUGHT THEY'D NEVER FINISH DIGGING.

It was impossible. *Unthinkable.*

But night after night, week after week, shovelful after shovelful, something had taken shape. Something that grew larger and more elaborate, until Jory held his breath every time he saw it. Because even though it terrified him, he felt an irresistible sense of *accomplishment.*

His family had created a bunker.

A shelter.

All by themselves.

As far as space went, it wasn't very big. About twice the size of their kitchen, with a low ceiling Jory could brush his fingertips across.

Crossbeams reinforced the ceiling, braced by two-by-fours jammed into the dirt walls. The family had packed hundreds of rocks into the walls between them—all the rocks Kit had sorted.

For storage, the family had carved a large hollow into the west wall, half again as large as the main space itself. Rows of empty shelves filled it, anticipating the tubs of supplies.

Against the south wall, three heavy boards topped with foam pads would serve as bunks. One for Mom and Caleb. One for Jory and Ansel. One for Kit.

They'd have no electricity, of course. Battery-powered lanterns hung from hooks screwed into the crossbeams. For cooking, Caleb had rigged a propane stove under an air shaft. They would mostly use it for boiling water, he said.

The bathroom was a nook where the north and east walls met. Inside, they'd dug a deep pit, with a board suspended over it and a second air shaft overhead. For flushing, a valve spilled water into the pit, and a drainpipe carried everything into the ravine. A shower curtain created a semblance of privacy. But Jory couldn't imagine doing his business there, with the rest of the family right outside. Or showering, because the nook was for washing, too.

He couldn't imagine himself anywhere inside the bunker, really.

Except for one place.

In the very center of the room, Mom had placed an old card table and five folding chairs. Whenever Jory looked at it, he saw himself sitting there until his hair turned gray and his skin turned white, paled by the darkness.

—

On Sunday, Jory volunteered to set the table, even though it seemed pointless now. Dinner wasn't worth any sort of fanfare: a smorgasbord of cottage cheese, stale bread, old raisins, and dried-up baby carrots. The dregs of the perishables. But preparing it had taken Mom as long as a cooking a four-course meal.

She had another migraine.

Jory recognized the ache in her face, even though she tried to hide it. Every line seemed deeper, especially the ones around her eyes. And her hands shook, which was most telling of all. It reminded Jory of that moment in the coffee shop, when she'd dropped the tray of mugs. The explosive instant that had brought the family together.

The moment that had started it all.

Jory glanced at Ansel and Kit. They played at the kitchen table, seemingly oblivious: Kit tweaking Ansel's ears and pinching at his nose, Ansel giggling delightedly. Neither had been around back then. Only Jory remembered.

What if Mom *hadn't* had a migraine that day? Or if she'd managed to carry the coffee to the tables? For that matter, what if Dad hadn't left for the city in the first place? What if he'd brought Mom and Jory along?

Life would have turned out entirely different.

But you couldn't play *what if* games with your memories, Jory knew. Because they'd already happened.

Crash!

He whirled around. A jar had slipped from Mom's hands, scattering glass and glossy red peppers across the floor. Ansel mashed his fists into his eyes and began to cry.

"Don't move," Mom said. "There's glass all over the place—I'll clean it up, just . . ."

"I've got it," Jory said, reaching for the broom.

Caleb appeared in the doorway. "What happened?" He glanced at Mom, whose fingertips were pressed against her temples. "Are you all right?"

She nodded, then grimaced. As if even that small movement brought more pain.

"She has a migraine," Jory said.

"I'm fine," she murmured.

"No you're not, Mom. You should be in bed. We should *all* be in bed. We're so tired. . . ."

Jory bit his lip to shut himself up. Caleb glanced from Mom to Kit, who was leaning against the counter. She straightened. But the shadows under her eyes said enough. He glanced at Ansel, who wailed and wailed.

"Go to bed," Caleb ordered Mom.

"But I'm fine, really. There's so much more to—"

"I insist."

She set the dishtowel on the counter and shuffled away.

Maybe Jory shouldn't have told on her, but she looked so frail. Same with Kit. And Ansel, who was still crying. His face wasn't quite plum-colored—maybe maroon?—but it still looked alarming. Jory leaned down to pick him up, but he twisted away.

"He wants his father," Caleb said, scooping up Ansel.

But Ansel continued to cry. He wriggled against Caleb, stretching out his dimpled baby arms.

Toward Kit.

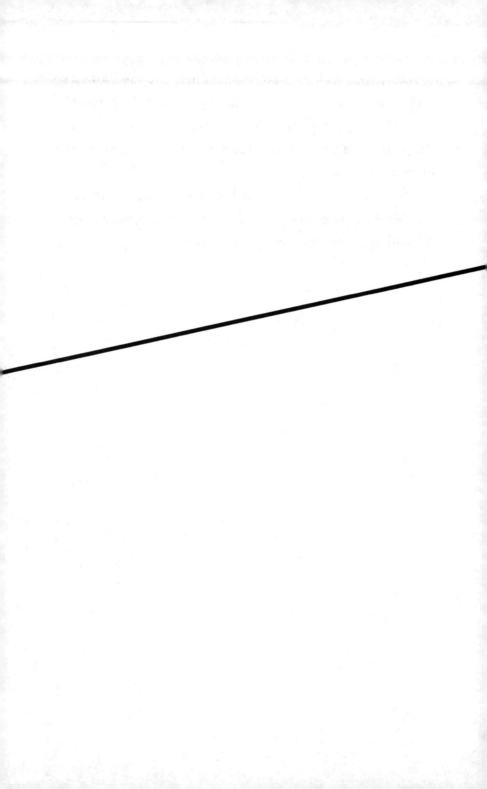

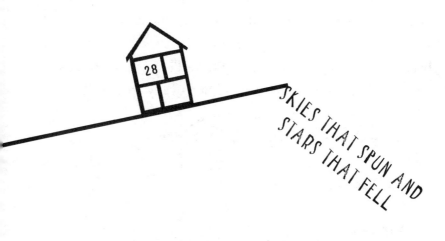

SKIES THAT SPUN AND STARS THAT FELL

THE NIGHT WAS THE PURPLE KIND: shades of navy and mauve and deep-violet, crinkling into the foliage, collecting in pools between piles of dirt. In the early winter chill, crickets were few.

Danger was brewing.

Jory felt it whenever Caleb glanced at Kit. Whenever Kit glanced at Caleb. Whenever Caleb glanced at Jory—just an expressionless glance, not a glare. But every single time it happened, Jory felt like cringing. Like digging a hole and covering himself up. He couldn't believe he'd talked back to Caleb last night. That he'd challenged his stepdad's leadership.

In a sense, Ansel reaching for Kit was the same thing.

Jory worked with his shoulders hunched in nervous anticipation—not for a sudden certainty, but for something bad to happen.

It didn't take long.

Kit was helping Jory hide another air shaft when it happened. Her shovel punched into a centipede nest. There were *thousands* of them. Or maybe it just seemed that way because of all the wicked-looking legs. They poured out like a wriggling geyser, some of them practically springing into the air in their fury to escape.

"Gross," Jory said cheerfully. "That's not a surprise you want to—"

Kit began to scream.

And scream.

And *scream*.

She'd never spoken in front of Mom and Caleb. She'd never cried or laughed or even whimpered. And now her voice echoed through the canyon, sharp and high and almost deafening.

She screamed so loudly the entire family was shocked stiff for a moment. Then Jory, Mom, and Caleb all lunged for her at the same time. Mom caught her first, but Kit twisted loose. She hurled her shovel into the brush, and screamed, and *screamed*.

Jory clasped a gloved hand over her mouth. "Shhh," he hissed. "Kit, you'll wake the neighbors."

But she wouldn't listen. She kept whimpering into his glove, squirming and thrashing, her ankles pounding his shins.

"Please," Mom pleaded. "Honey, *please!*"

But Kit was inconsolable. Again, she broke free. Her voice rose into a high-pitched shriek—silenced by a smack across the face. The force of Caleb's gloved hand sent her flailing backward into a patch of creosote.

"Listen here, girl," he said while Kit cried soundlessly. "Your mother and I are saving your life. We owe you nothing—absolutely nothing. You should be grateful. Hear me?"

Mom was crying too. Jory tried to catch her eyes, but they remained on Kit. So did Ansel's—even though just yesterday, he'd reached for her first. But Caleb's stare was the most intense of all. Like instead of a nine-year-old girl, a wild animal crouched there in the brush.

Undomesticated.

Untrustworthy.

—

The rest of the night passed in a blur. Caleb hauled Kit out of the canyon and put her to bed, the rest of the family hot on their heels. Ansel, too. He started bawling a second after the slap and wouldn't quit, no matter how Mom tried to console him.

Only Caleb and Jory returned to the canyon that night. They worked in heavy silence. Jory wanted to ask his step-dad questions, but he was afraid. Afraid of Caleb's angry eyes. Afraid of the revelations beneath his thick, dark beard.

Afraid of his gloved hand.

By now, the centipedes had all scampered away. Jory finished hiding the air shaft by himself. He kept glancing down at Caleb, who was replanting shrubs to look more natural. It was a delicate job, but Caleb found every excuse to slash at the dirt with his shovel. Jory winced at every snap of roots, every violent crunch of earth.

When they returned home, Jory had trouble sleeping. He kept thinking of Kit's shrieks, the way they echoed through the canyon. The way Jory could almost hear *words* in the sound: those sentences that, for whatever reason, Kit hadn't been able to say.

I don't care what's coming!

I don't want to get buried alive!

Even when he finally slept, the sounds followed him into his dreams. Dreams of skies that spun and stars that fell. Dreams of sunshine inked over by blackness. Dreams of the end of his world.

—

Early the next morning, Mom came into Jory's room. Her expression made the room stagger and sway. "They took her," she said.

"They took who?

Mom just stared at him, her eyes shining with tears.

"Kit? They took Kit?"

She nodded. "The people in suits. Caleb tried to stop

them, but—they had papers, Jory." She sobbed. "They had *papers*."

"Officials?"

She nodded again. "They said they could arrest us all if we didn't give her up."

Jory thought of the Officials who'd come to his door before. The man with glasses. The woman with the badge. *No!* He tried to swing his legs out of bed, but they got tangled in the covers. He shoved at them, his hands shaking violently, his chest aflame. "But I didn't—why didn't I hear it? Why didn't you wake me up?"

Another sob shook her. "He said it all happened so fast."

"Where'd they take her? It's not too late—you can't just *take* somebody. . . ." Finally, the covers fell away. "We have to find her, Mom!"

She reached for him, but he ducked away and ran down the hall. "Kit!" he called, stumbling over his own feet and nearly toppling down the stairs.

He burst outside and into the fields. The sky was the palest pink. A delicate, lovely color, which was absolutely wrong. Didn't the sky know the world was ending? He called Kit's name again and again, at the top of his lungs.

Then he tripped over a pumpkin vine and landed hard. Pain shuddered through his knees. Caleb reached him seconds later.

"Get ahold of yourself!" he shouted, shaking Jory by the shoulders.

"We've got to go after her!" Jory sobbed. "We've got to stop them, they can't be that far—we've got to save her. . . ."

"Lower your voice." Caleb released him. "I'm sorry, Jory, but it's too late. I lied the best I could, but the Officials had papers. There was nothing I could do for her without putting the rest of us in danger. They could have taken you and Ansel, too."

"But . . ." How could Caleb give her up, just like that? Why was he acting so *calm* about it? "We can't just . . . We have to do something!"

"There was nothing I could do for her," Caleb said again.

Mom knelt beside Jory. She wrapped her arms around him and rubbed his back, rocking him, their tears soaking each other's neck and shoulders.

"I need you to be strong, my love," she said. "For me. For your brother. Because we *are* doing something. We're saving ourselves."

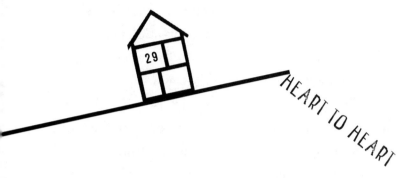

HEART TO HEART

THEY WERE ALMOST OUT OF TIME.

The Officials could return any day, Caleb said. Any moment. The family—what was left of the family—worked all night. And the next. For once, Jory was thankful for the hard work. Thankful for the dark.

It made it much, much easier not to think. Because when he did think, his thoughts were filled with Kit. Where she'd gone. Who had taken her. If he'd ever see her again.

What it meant for the rest of Caleb's predictions.

Whether they'd all come true, too.

The bunker was finished. Only supplies were left—many of them too large to carry down the trail. So they loaded Caleb's truck and drove it to another entrance to the canyon, by the bridge.

The truck could make it halfway down this slope, which

was less steep. Still, dragging the trailer the rest of the way sapped every ounce of strength in Jory's tired body. Even with all three of them working together. It hardly helped, of course, that Ansel rode on top. But Jory didn't complain.

He didn't speak at all.

There was nothing left to say.

The family filled the bunker sack by sack. Tub by tub. They filled it with innumerable boxes of candles, soap, cloth diapers for Ansel, paper towels and real towels, cans of food, lemon-scented baby wipes to keep the family lemon-scented. Flashlights, lanterns, batteries, sleeping bags and blankets, toiletries and first aid, emergency, defense.

And boulders. For sealing themselves inside, when the time came.

The water drums were the worst, though. Each weighed hundreds of pounds. Eight pounds to a gallon, Caleb said. And the gallons were endless. All day long, they filled the drums with a garden hose. Jory wondered what their water bill would look like.

Then he realized it wouldn't matter, after.

When they reached the mouth of their shelter, they rolled each drum down the trailer's tailgate and into the bunker. It was exhausting. And painful. Jory's arms felt like spaghetti. His legs felt like pudding. But, somehow, he did it.

Somehow, they finished.

On his way out—the last time, before their final

return—Jory stopped and stared at the empty card table. The shelter had seemed larger, somehow, when there was nothing in it. After filling it to the brim with supplies, it felt suffocating. A madhouse of objects, a turbulent swirl of *stuff*.

Even so, it was hard to believe it was enough to sustain the family for three months, much less six.

Though the family was one person smaller now.

—

By the time Jory woke up the next day, it was afternoon. Caleb wasn't home, so Jory joined Mom and Ansel at the kitchen table. A somber, silent trio.

Since they'd packed all the food in the kitchen, Mom made MREs once again: Caleb's soldier meals. Jory poked at his glumly. Their novelty had long since worn off. Mom poked at hers, too. He wondered if she was thinking about Kit.

A mother's love is an invisible cord, she'd said, *linking her children heart to heart.*

He wondered where Kit was right now.

Maybe in a jail, like the one where the officers put Caleb—where they mocked him and laughed at him and spit in his food. But that jail was for soldiers, not for little girls.

In an orphanage, where she had to beg for gruel.

At a training camp for Officials and officers.

Or maybe she'd tipped back her head, spread her arms, and leaped into the sky. He pictured her soaring through the stars, a girl-shaped meteor, her laughter tickling the ears of the startled Officials. For a moment, he almost smiled.

Rap. Rap. Rap.

Mom and Jory stared at each other. "Do you want me to—" he began.

"Don't be silly," Mom said, touching Ansel. His lower lip quivered, but he didn't cry.

"Can't we just ignore it?"

She pushed her chair back from the table. "We shouldn't," she said, patting down her braid. "I'll just tell them Caleb's not home. Whoever it is."

Jory waited apprehensively. Could it be the Officials again? For a split second, he wished they hadn't already packed the DEFENSE tub in the canyon.

"It's okay," Mom said when she returned. "It's just that girl. The one in the plaid jacket. I don't mind if you say your good-byes, but be quick."

Jory knew Mom was being kind, but he didn't want to talk to Alice. "That's okay. You can tell her I'm busy."

"Jory . . ." Mom gazed at him for a moment, like she couldn't find the words she wanted. "Just talk to her. You'll regret it if you don't."

He nodded, sighed, and went.

Alice stood there with her plaid arms crossed, chewing on her lip. "Hi, Jory."

He waved two fingers.

"Mr. Bradley says you're gonna be homeschooled again," Alice said. "Is that true?"

"For now."

"At least you won't have to deal with all the human wastes anymore. We've got double our share at school, that's for sure."

Jory didn't say anything. Alice looked even more nervous.

"So . . . is Kit around?" she asked.

"She's gone."

"What do you mean, gone? Where is she?"

"The Officials took her."

"The Officials? Like . . . the police? Or . . ."

"Why don't you ask your mom?"

Alice gaped at him. "My mom? What . . ." Then realization dawned on her face. Instead of shoving back her cuffs, she pulled them over her hands. "I didn't mean to . . . My mom and I are really close. We share almost everything. I only told her because I was worried, because you said Kit was sick, and she hadn't been to a doctor, and I—I didn't think she'd tell anyone, Jory! I really didn't. I'm so sorry."

Jory bit the inside of his cheeks. Right now, he didn't feel angry. Just heavy.

"It's okay if you don't want to talk to me. I understand." Alice took a deep breath. "But I want you to know that I'll be here. If you're ever ready to be friends again."

Friends.

The word revved his heartbeat. It made him feel like he was whooshing down hills and breathing eucalyptus. Standing at the edge of the world and reaching toward the sky.

He hadn't wanted to tell Alice anything.

Now he wanted to tell her everything.

About the canyon, and the bunker, and the danger from above but also all around them. That he was scared, so scared, because he didn't know what was true. The danger might be real. The Officials had *taken* his *sister.*

Jory didn't want to be buried alive.

But he knew he couldn't have both, the possibilities of the daylight and the safety underground. He couldn't have friends and family, too.

And he'd chosen his family.

"Good-bye, Alice," Jory said.

He shut the door.

Mom was waiting for him in the kitchen. She looked young and old all at once, and very, very sad. "Oh, Jory," she said. "All I've ever wanted is to keep you safe."

When *Mom* said that, Jory believed her. "What about Kit?" he asked.

"We'll get her back," Mom said softly. "I promise we will."

Hope sparked in Jory's chest. "When?"

"It'll have to be after."

He hesitated, then nodded. Then he leaned over and hugged her. "I love you, Mom," he said.

She hugged him back.

Jory didn't have Kit to protect anymore, but he could still protect Mom—just like she'd tried to protect him.

No matter what happened.

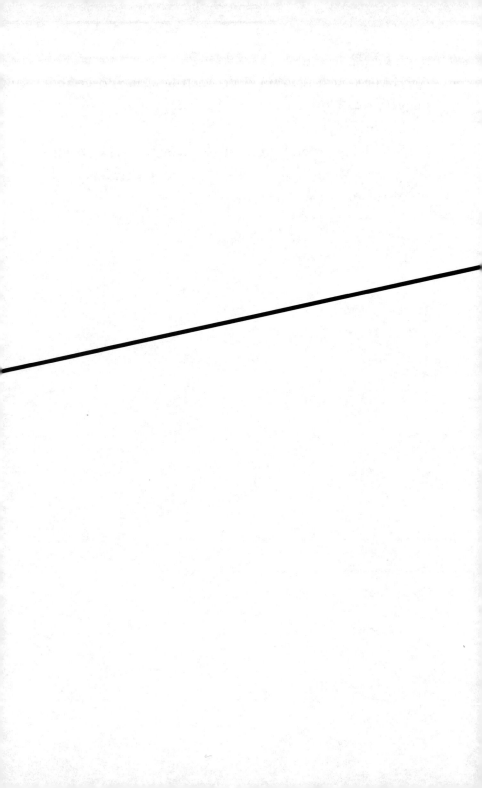

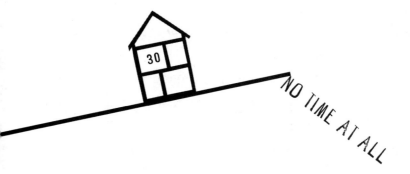

NO TIME AT ALL

THE FAMILY PREPARED THE HOUSE CAREFULLY FOR THEIR DEPARTURE.
They cleaned the kitchen with soap and bleach, sanitizing every surface as best as they could by lantern light. They swept the floors three times and dumped the dustpan in the fields. They made their beds with military precision, smoothing every last wrinkle out of their pillows while Caleb observed.

"What about Kit's room?" Jory asked.

Caleb waved his hand dismissively. "It doesn't matter. The Officials know she's not with us."

"But—" Jory began.

"Don't forget to get the mail," Caleb said. "We don't want to tip off the mailperson that we're missing before we're ready. Although they'll know soon enough. Can you imagine what it'll be like? When the Officials realize we're gone? When they knock on our door and no one answers? The beds all nicely made—Oh, it'll be a riot. Too bad we won't be here to see it."

His eyes weren't just smiling, but *beaming*. He picked up Ansel and swung him around.

"Nobody would ever think in a million years we were just a short hike away, safe and sound underground, waiting for the marvelous after."

"After . . ." Jory began.

Caleb set down Ansel and looked at Jory. "Yes?"

"After it's all . . ." He swallowed. "Are we coming back here?"

"I'm sure we'll want to stop by—for a good old-fashioned shower, at least, as long as the pipes are still in working order."

"But we won't be living here?"

"I don't think so. Why would we? We'll be able to take our pick of any house in town." Caleb patted Jory's shoulder. "I'll bet you even have one in mind."

He couldn't help it—he thought of Alice's house, with its yellow curtains and ancient computers. She was planning on moving to a new house anyway, wasn't she? He thought of the blue farmhouse down the street that looked so much like theirs. He thought of the neighbor ladies' house across the canyon, and Panda breaking free of their fence.

"Not really," Jory said. "Where will everybody else go?"

"Don't you worry about that," Caleb said.

But how could Jory not? How could *Caleb* not? Not trusting other people was one thing. But not caring if they lived or—or whatever he thought might happen to them?

That was another.

And what did that mean for Kit? Caleb had *promised* to keep her safe—but already it was like he'd forgotten her. Like he wasn't even worried about her.

Like she'd never really mattered to him at all.

The family waited as Caleb thought long and hard about whether to leave a light on. "It might take the Officials longer to realize we're missing," he mused. "But then again, it might draw them to the house. If they knock, they'll think we're ignoring them."

"Either way, your truck will be here," Mom pointed out.

"True."

In the end, Caleb decided to leave one lamp on, beside the front door.

"Now what?" Jory asked.

"Now we wait."

———

Jory headed to Kit's room instead of his.

It was dark, but he didn't want to turn on a light. He lifted the blinds. First a bit, then all the way. A wedge of moonlight brightened the room, just enough to see her bedside table, her flowered blanket. Her broken, filthy ballet slippers nestled in one corner.

Jory couldn't bring himself to pick them up.

He turned back to her window. So *this* was what Kit saw when she looked outside. The window faced a different direction than his. Not the canyon, but the rest of the world. More sky, out that way. The way from which she came, which Jory still knew barely anything about. Wherever she might be right now.

Suddenly, Jory saw movement in the fields. His heart skipped a beat.

But it was just a bird—a blackbird, he thought, or maybe a mockingbird. It fluttered and landed, fluttered and landed, then hopped onto the mailbox for a few seconds before taking off into the dark.

The mailbox! He'd forgotten to get the mail.

Jory slipped from Kit's room and hurried down the stairs. Outside, he jogged across the fields toward the road.

The mailbox creaked as he opened it. It was too dark to see, so he felt around inside. No letters—just a brick.

A brick?

He pulled it out. It wasn't a brick; it was something hard and brick-shaped, wrapped in brown paper. Almost a dozen stamps were stuck on it, crooked and overlapping. Underneath the stamps, was written JORY BIRCH. And the family's address. Nothing else.

Jory stared at it for a moment. What in the world? Then he tucked it under his arm and ran for the house. In the shadows beside the porch, he tore it open.

It was one of their Worldbuilding houses.

He peered at it more closely, then held it out so the moonlight could catch it. She'd worked on it since he'd last seen it: now the walls were green, blue, yellow, and orange—one of each. On the roof, she'd painted a constellation of red stars. She'd used a pen to draw tiny, spiky flowers around the bottom. An itty-bitty dog looked out the window, with its paws on the sill. Black and white, like Panda.

"I thought you didn't like him," Jory whispered.

He turned the house over and found a message.

I AM FINE.

In big, bold capital letters, penmanship as shiny bright as Kit's voice. Tears sprang to Jory's eyes. He cradled the house against his chest, feeling worse and better.

But mostly better.

Kit loved the sky and the sun and the stars. She *needed* them. She didn't want to be buried. *Couldn't* be buried. As long as she was in reach of the sky . . . she'd be okay. Jory didn't need a sign to tell him that. Whatever happened— whatever *had* happened, that day the Officials came—Kit would be okay.

She'd be fine.

If only Jory could say the same for himself.

—

Jory returned to his room and waited in the dark. It seemed like eternity. It seemed like no time at all. The minutes kept rushing around him, one after the other, spinning like a whirlpool with the moon at the bottom. Finally, he heard a knock on his door.

"Come in," Jory said, expecting Mom.

It was Caleb.

"It's time," he said. "It's time."

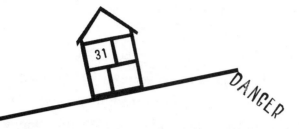

31

THE NIGHT SMELLED ELECTRIC.

"A storm's coming," Mom whispered, hugging Ansel against her. She'd bundled him into his down jacket and a crocheted cap. His round-cheeked face peered out sleepily.

Jory wiped the prickly feeling from his nose with a numb hand. Everything felt dreamlike: the *skree* of crickets, the impossible weight of the navy-gray sky. It could all be a movie he was watching about somebody else. But the scent made it real.

"We'll be underground before the rain falls," Caleb said.

"You're absolutely certain no water can get in?" Mom asked, looking nervous.

Caleb locked the back door and dropped the key in his pocket. "Of course I'm sure. I tested it."

"How, exactly? I'm not sure you ever—"

"Don't worry," he said, cutting her off. "But we should hurry—we don't want to get caught outside." He nodded at the sky. "The storm might be the beginning."

"Of what?" Jory asked.

"Of the danger."

Danger. A word you never could get used to. It echoed in Jory's head as they walked away from the house. *Danger.* As he stumbled through the canyon like a marionette, floppy and limp-limbed. *Danger. Danger. Danger.* If Jory thought it enough times, maybe it would become meaningless.

Instead, it sounded like an alarm.

Jory had been taught not to trust anybody but his family. Especially not the Officials. And just like Caleb had warned, the Officials had taken Kit away.

But Kit was fine.

He thought again of the Officials who'd knocked on his door. The curly-haired woman who'd given him her card. The sharp-toothed man who'd searched for candy in his pockets. At the time, they'd seemed so sinister.

But what if they weren't? What if that had just been Caleb peering over Jory's shoulder? Inhabiting Jory's skin?

What if the Officials weren't the enemy after all?

The family hiked down the ravine, like they had so many times before. But with the storm at his back, Jory couldn't stop imagining it filled with rushing water. Was the bunker really waterproof? *Don't worry,* Caleb had said. But Jory worried.

As they squeezed through the chaparral thicket, the bunker appeared in the brush like a hungry dark mouth. Jory could swear he felt heat radiating from inside.

Danger. "We've arrived," Caleb said. "This is it."

Mom and Jory and Ansel stayed silent.

A dog began to bark. Panda? Would he still be there, after?

What else would be left? Their house? All the stuff they didn't bring into the canyon? Jory thought of the marks on the doorjamb where Mom had documented their height. He had grown almost a foot in the last few years. Kit had only grown an inch or two. Ansel hadn't been standing all that long, so he only had a couple of lines.

Would they keep growing underground? Or would they wither and shrink, like plants shut away from the light?

"Time to say good-bye," Caleb said, pinching Ansel's cheeks. "Good-bye to all the houses and trees. Good-bye to the stars."

But there weren't any stars. The clouds covered them all. Another meteor shower could be exploding through the sky—a sign they should turn back, tuck themselves into bed and forget the bunker—and they wouldn't even know it.

Jory thought of the neighbor ladies and their blueberry scones.

He thought of Mr. Bradley and the tunnels project he would never hand in.

He thought of Alice Brooks-Diaz, whose feelings he'd

hurt so badly—and she forgave him anyway. It made him want to cry, thinking of that kindness. She'd only wanted to help Kit, after all. And so had Alice's mom. He knew that now.

He felt the dampness in the air and its threat of coming rain. The grinning bunker, beckoning them closer. And the darn dog! Who kept barking.

And barking.

And barking, until Jory wanted to cover his ears. Because it, too, sounded like an alarm. He was standing at the brink of darkness, all alone with his family, *Danger* whirling all around him. *Danger* in the storm above. *Danger* in the ground below.

"All right, my family," Caleb said. "Shall we go in?"

He held a hand out to Mom. She hesitated for a second, then joined him, hugging Ansel tight. "Jory?" she said glancing over her shoulder. "You ready?"

Jory wanted to join them. He wanted to believe them. But he kept standing there, his stomach tight.

He was in the canyon. But he was also hovering above it, gazing down at his tiny family. He thought of his dreams of darkness. Of the last star going out.

And suddenly, it washed over him in a hot, shimmering wave: the overwhelming certainty he'd always waited for, but never felt. Not with the whited-out newspaper, or the meteor shower, or the five dead birds Caleb had found in a row—if the birds had even existed, since nobody but Caleb had seen them. Not even when Jory had glimpsed the bright red star late at night.

Suddenly, Jory knew.

"No," he said.

"No?" Caleb repeated.

"No, I'm not ready. I'm not—I'm not going."

There was a moment of silence. The seconds throbbed against Jory's temples.

"Jory . . ." Mom said, her voice shrill and panicked. "Of course you're coming with us. We're your family."

Jory shook his head.

Caleb exhaled. A small hurricane of frustration. "Boy, now's not the time to hesitate. We've had weeks to discuss this. Don't be ridiculous."

"*Please,*" Mom begged.

"No," Jory said again. And then he said it louder. "*No.* I'm not going in there. And neither should you, Mom."

Her eyes welled up. "I'm not letting our family get split up again."

She meant Kit. When Kit had been taken. Now Jory understood.

"You don't want to split up the family?" He pointed at Caleb. "*He* split up the family! He lied about Kit, Mom. Protective Services took Kit away. Not to hurt her, but to *protect* her. From *us.*"

The wind picked up, chattering through the underbrush.

The electricity in the air made his skin prickle and the hair on his arms stand on end.

"Protective Services?" Mom repeated. "But how—"

"I called them," Caleb said.

She stared at him. "You called Protective Services?"

"I told them we'd found her in our pumpkin field—that we'd only just now found her. It's not like she has the ability to tell them otherwise."

"But *why*?"

"You knew as well as I did that Kit was going wild. Keeping her was always a risk. But her behavior has been too unpredictable lately. Too dangerous." Caleb shook his head, looking contrite. "It's regrettable, but I had to think of the rest of the family. Especially Ansel. Remember, Kit was never ours. Not like Ansel is."

And not like Jory. Who wasn't Caleb's real son either.

Jory knew blood didn't necessarily make a family—Dad wasn't part of his family anymore, and Kit *was*. But both sides had to want it. Both sides had to feel it.

Jory was only family when he followed Caleb's orders.

"That's not true!" Jory exclaimed. "You're a liar!"

Caleb's eyes blazed. "If somehow you survive this, in the world after, we'll *never* forgive you." He placed a hand on Mom's shoulder. "It's time to go."

Mom pushed his hand away. "No."

"What did you say?"

She looked at him, her eyes wet and bright and almost as

large as Kit's. "You said you'd keep her safe. You *promised*."

This silence lasted even longer than the one before. Caleb's palms were open, his arms curved. A circle, but only half complete. "You're giving up on your family."

"Jory and Kit are my family too. A whole half of it. I can't abandon them to save myself. If it's even . . ." Her chin trembled. "If we even know . . ."

"Know what?"

"That the danger's real," she said.

Caleb laughed. A sound like bat wings flapping. "Of course it's real! I've spent every second of every minute of every hour for *years* now confirming it—we're in danger, it's coming, it's *real*. We need to go. Let's go."

Mom shook her head.

"*Now!*" His voice bellowed through the canyon. Mom kept shaking her head. Caleb advanced on her. But he didn't reach for Mom.

He reached for Ansel.

"No!" Mom exclaimed, backing away. "You're not taking him."

Caleb kept moving toward her, his huge hands raised, every crease embedded with dirt. His chest heaved. "He needs me."

"*No!*"

"I'm your father," Caleb said to Ansel. He made a swipe for him, but only caught his shoe. Ansel began to cry.

Jory started toward them, then stumbled over a root. He

glanced down. It wasn't a root—it was Kit's shovel. She'd hurled it into the brush the night she'd found the centipede nest. His fingers curled tightly around the shovel's ice-cold handle.

"I'm taking him," Caleb said. "And there's nothing you can do."

"I won't let you." Jory held up Kit's shovel.

Caleb looked startled, then amused. "You don't speak for this family, boy."

"Neither do you."

"I'm the head of the family—"

"Why, because you said so?"

"Because everything I do is for the family, can't you *see*?" Caleb was shouting even louder now. "The birds! The five dead birds . . . and the stars! I didn't make that up! Those were signs, and so was the *newspaper*, and if we don't go underground now, we'll never be safe. You *need* me—"

"No we don't," Mom said.

Jory raised the shovel.

Caleb backed away, until he stood at the entrance to the bunker, staring at the family. *His* family. Jory, gripping the shovel. Mom, unsteady beside him. Ansel, crying in her arms. Caleb looked tall and fierce and proud, and for an instant, Jory felt a flash of what he'd felt at the coffee shop, years ago—*this man could protect us from anything.*

Then Caleb ducked inside.

One by one, he rolled the boulders into the opening.

Slowly, because he had no help. His bearded face became a pale triangle.

Then he pulled the rip cord.

An avalanche of earth tumbled down, until black met black and nothing remained. Just a cloud of dust drifting into the night sky. A heap of rocks and weeds and roots, blending into the natural disarray of the canyon.

The bunker was gone.

And so was Caleb.

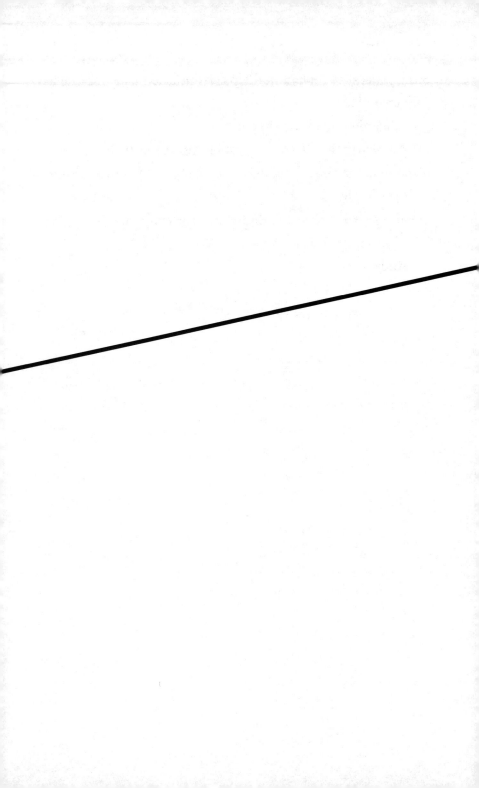

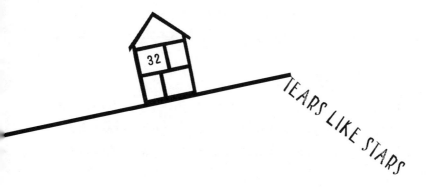

32

TEARS LIKE STARS

THE FAMILY STOOD THERE A WHILE LONGER, clinging to each other. Mom wept silently, her tears like stars. Ansel gazed up at her, his fingers in his mouth. Jory wondered how much his brother understood. Maybe more than they realized.

The shovel felt hot in Jory's hands. He jammed it crookedly into the earth. In that moment, it felt like something had severed—the imaginary cords that had bound them to Caleb. Ankle to ankle, maybe, but never heart to heart.

"Let's go home," Jory said. "And in the morning . . ."

Mom smiled at him shakily, her chin resting on Ansel's head. "In the morning, I'll make some phone calls. Okay?"

"You will?"

"Of course." She took Jory's hand.

"She's fine. I *know* she is. And we'll be . . ." He paused. When he thought about it, he realized he knew lots of people they could go to for help. They weren't alone. Not this time. "We'll be fine too."

The first gray light brightened the horizon. Jory hesitated, looking toward the place where the entrance to the bunker had been. He listened.

From the earth, he heard nothing.

From the sky, however, he thought he heard a faint rumbling. Thunder, maybe? Or the pounding of his own head. His heart. Mom squeezed his hand, and he turned away.

Together, they began to climb.

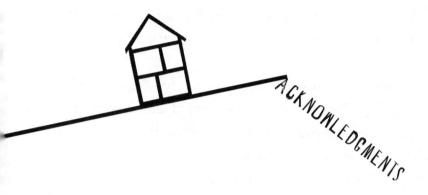

THIS BOOK IS DEDICATED TO MY TWIN SISTER, Danielle, and all those shared childhood books that wore our (tough) love like velveteen rabbits; stories that will reside forever in our bones.

Other important thanks:

My brilliant agent, Michelle Andelman, and the team at Regal Literary, Inc.

Emily Meehan, my editor at Disney-Hyperion, along with Jessica Harriton, Jenica Nasworthy, designer Whitney Manger, artist and photographer David Hughes, and art director Joann Hill for crafting a cover that so breathtakingly captures Jory's story.

My family, the Hubbards and the Allens, especially my dear Bryson; and all my quirky, delightful, supportive friends. My critique partners Michelle Schusterman, Kaitlin

Ward, Kate Hart, Sarah Enni, Kristin Halbrook, Phoebe North, and Stephanie Kuehn, along with the other authors at YA Highway (past and present) for unconditional love, humor, and inspiration. I'll bet you're made of more than 93 percent stardust.

Watch the Sky began its life ten years ago as a short story; it won UCSD's Milton H. Saier Award, and was the first work of fiction I was ever paid for. Many thanks to Eileen Myles, whose encouragement helped keep the story in my head until it was ready to unearth and expand.

Last but not least, the canyons of Southern California, which I've grown to know so well: their scents and sounds, the way they look at night . . . and all the secrets that might be hidden there.